ELIZABETH AND ZENOBIA

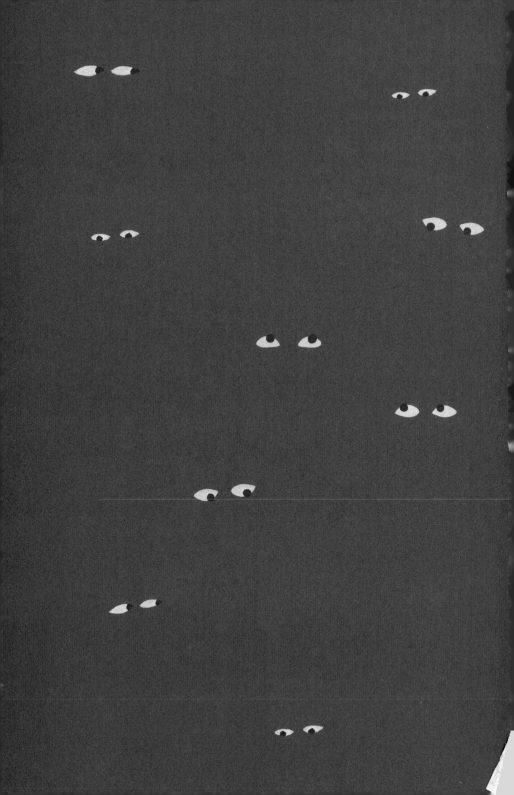

ELIZABETH
AND
ZENOBIA

Jessica Miller

AMULET BOOKS
NEW YORK

Cataloging-in-Publication Data has been applied for and may be obtained from the Library of Congress.

ISBN 978-1-4197-2724-5

Text copyright © 2016 Jessica Miller

Jacket illustrations copyright © 2017 Yelena Bryksenkova

Book design by Alyssa Nassner and Tree Abraham

Lines of poetry quoted on pages 43–44 are from "The Raven" (1845) by Edgar Allan Poe; page 50, "The Complaint: or Night Thoughts on Life, Death, and Immortality" (1742–46), also known as "Night Thoughts," by Edward Young; page 50, "The Grave" (1745) by Robert Blair; pages 126–127, "The Lady of Shalott" (1832) by Alfred, Lord Tennyson.

First published by the Text Publishing Company in Melbourne, Australia, in 2016.

Amulet Books and Amulet Paperbacks are registered trademarks of Harry N. Abrams, Inc.

Printed and bound in USA

10 9 8 7 6 5 4 3 2 1

Amulet Books are available at special discounts when purchased in quantity for premiums and promotions as well as fundraising or educational use. Special editions can also be created to specification. For details, contact specialsales@abramsbooks.com or the address below.

ABRAMS The Art of Books
115 West 18th Street, New York, NY 10011
abramsbooks.com

Witheringe House

itheringe House. That was the name of the
new house. Though it wasn't new, really. It had
been Father's when he was a child.

Still, it was new to me.

I had never been there. All I knew of it was the name.

Witheringe House.

I have always paid attention to words and the way they fill my
ears. There are words I could hear over and over again, like "sea-
shell." And there are other words, like "custard," that make my
stomach flip. Witheringe House. I tried it in my mind and found
I couldn't enjoy it. The sound of it was too much like—

"Like a withered limb." Zenobia finished the sentence for
me. "Like an apple left in the sun, turned soft and small."

"I wish you wouldn't do that," I told her.

"I can't help it," she said.

It was true, she couldn't. Zenobia didn't read minds, exactly, but sometimes other people's thoughts passed through her, unbidden. "The same as a shiver," she had said when she described it to me.

"Like a shriveled head," she said now, softly.

I turned to look down the length of Platform Seven. "Father's taking a long time with the tickets," I said. "And I can't see him at all, not in this . . ."

I waved a hand at the fog, cold and gray and velvet, hanging over the platform. "I could see him over the crowd a moment ago, but now . . ." I stood on my trunk and tried to find Father's black bowler hat bobbing above the heads of the passengers waiting to board. "Now I've lost him."

Zenobia clasped at the grayness with her thin white hands and gathered it close. "I think there is something deliciously bleak about fog, don't you, Elizabeth?"

"No. And the train leaves in seven minutes, and if—"

"I wish I could keep a scrap of fog in my pocket for whenever the weather got oppressively nice."

I went up on tiptoe, but there was still no black hat to be seen.

The train at Platform Eight pulled away, and smoke mixed with the fog. I covered my ears against the heavy, creaking sound the train made leaving the station. When the creaking faded, I heard another noise.

Someone whistling. A light, cascading tune.

It filled me with dread.

"Listen," I hissed, and Zenobia did.

She frowned. "It's the aria from—"

"From *The Magic Flute*," I finished. "I hope Father's not in earshot."

Zenobia nodded gravely. "Hearing that tune in his present condition—well—it may prove the last straw," she said.

Our train arrived. The waiting passengers became a surging crowd that elbowed and pushed and waved tickets in the air. Still no Father. Maybe he had gone and left me behind, just as Mother had done.

But then I saw the black hat and, underneath it, Father coming along the platform. His eyes slid over me, and he walked straight by. I wasn't surprised. I am small and quiet, the kind of girl it is easy to walk past without seeing.

I sprang down from my trunk, scraped past the woolen coats of the crowd, and caught at his sleeve.

"There you are, Elizabeth!" He turned and looked down at me. "The train's about to leave."

Aboard the train, in our compartment, Zenobia clicked open her silver pocket watch. "Eleven twenty-seven," she said. "Four minutes behind schedule."

I pressed my palm to the window. Outside, there was only

fog. I had planned to spend the journey looking through the glass, as the city unraveled into countryside. I had hoped—

"Yes, but it is Tuesday."

"Pardon?"

"You wanted to have your nose pressed up against the window all the way to Witheringe House, but you didn't account for the fact that it's Tuesday morning."

"And?"

"And," she finished, "Tuesday mornings are almost invariably gloomy."

I sighed. It was a shame, because I had hoped—

"Personally," she said, "I find fog more interesting to look at than fields or forests or rivers. They're all so dull—so utterly predictable. But fog! Anything could be hiding under this fog. It's got so much more potential."

I had hoped the sight of fields and forests and rivers might have cheered Father. He sat across from Zenobia and me. A book lay open on his lap, but his eyes weren't following the words across its pages, and his face was blank.

I wanted to ask Father about the new house and how he remembered it from when he was a boy. But I didn't want to intrude on his thoughts. Father hated being interrupted, and it had seemed particularly wise to leave him in peace since the evening Mother had failed to return from the opera.

After Mother left, Father didn't yell. He didn't cry. He just, somehow, stopped. He stopped going to work at the museum. He stopped writing articles about seed dispersal patterns in the dandelion genus, and he stopped dictating letters to the editors of the *Journal for Modern Biology*. Envelopes addressed to him lay unopened, and the *Times* lay unread beside his plate at breakfast.

I watched him and tried to decide if he felt angry. Or sad. Or nothing.

Three days after Mother left, I was at her dressing table. I was letting my fingers run very slowly across the pointed teeth of her hair comb. Zenobia came up behind me.

"She's never coming back, you know," she said.

I didn't want Zenobia to be right. But I remembered the night Mother left. She was wearing her emerald evening gown. Its sequins were like scales, and she flickered down the stairs like some kind of tropical fish. When she bent to brush her lips against my cheek, she stopped halfway and looked at me, confused. I think she had already started to forget who I was.

And then, a full twelve days later, there came a pink envelope with a note inside. Mother, as she explained in her flowing hand, had run off with the opera singer who understudied for the role of Tamino. She would follow *The Magic Flute* as it toured the opera houses of Europe. To Munich, Vienna, Prague, Bratislava. She had no plans to return.

I read the note when Father had finished with it, and I

believed every word, except for the two at the end where she signed herself off, "Love always."

A sharp rap came at the door of our compartment.

"Refreshments?" A man in a brocade waistcoat held the tea trolley steady. Father answered his question with a nod. The man set down a silver teapot and two cups on a table that unclipped from the wall. With silver tongs he placed a biscuit on each saucer.

Zenobia looked at the two cups and the two saucers and the two biscuits.

"Excuse me," I began, and the man in the waistcoat leaned in with one ear toward me to show he hadn't heard. I straightened in my seat and made my voice as loud as it would go.

"Excuse me," I said again, "but we need another cup."

Zenobia cleared her throat.

"And another biscuit," I finished.

Father put the ends of his fingers to his temples and closed his eyes. When he opened them, he said, "I hoped Zenobia might stay behind. Must she accompany us all the way to Witheringe Green?"

"I expect so," I told him, "as she is on the train with us now."

The man was looking at the gold buttons on his waistcoat.

"She's far too old for an imaginary friend, of course," Father said to him, "but perhaps you could humor her."

"Certainly, sir."

I saw the ends of the man's moustache twitch, but if he laughed at Zenobia or me, he waited until he had wheeled the trolley away.

"Imaginary friend indeed," muttered Zenobia while I poured her tea.

Zenobia is not imaginary at all. It is true no one except me can see her or hear her, but that doesn't mean I dreamed her up. Besides, as she so often likes to point out, it's unlikely that someone as dull or as timid as I could ever imagine someone like Zenobia.

But if she's not imaginary, she's not quite real either. For a start, Zenobia is pale. Very pale. Almost translucent in direct sunlight. And the irises of her eyes are black as tar. There's a faintness about her that makes it hard to tell where she ends and the rest of the world begins. And when she's upset or irritated, strange things—unnatural things—have a tendency to happen. It's like the thought-reading: she can't exactly help it. Or, at least, she says she can't—

"Urgh!" Father spat his mouthful of tea back into his cup. He used his handkerchief to wipe droplets of tea from his beard.

"I think," he said as he refolded the handkerchief, "there's something amiss with the tea."

"There is?" I looked into my cup. It seemed fine. I tasted it. It was fine.

"Yes, there is," he said. His face was still screwed up in disgust. "Perhaps it has been steeped too long."

I peered over the rim of his cup. It was filled with a thick black liquid. Bubbles formed, then burst across its surface. "Yes," I said, and I looked at Zenobia, who was looking up at the ceiling. "Perhaps that's it."

I finished my tea. Father let his go cold in front of him. Zenobia consulted her watch. "Twelve thirteen," she said. "Over three hours to go."

She pulled a book out of her pocket. It had a cardboard cover and its title read, in smudged type, *The World Beyond*. Under this, in smaller type, was *One Famed and Celebrated Clairvoyant's Guide to the World of the Spirits*. Underneath this, but in big letters, was the name of the Famed and Celebrated Clairvoyant herself: Madame Lucent.

Zenobia's latest obsession was clairvoyance.

When we were younger it had been anatomy, and Zenobia's pockets had rattled constantly with bird skulls and mouse bones.

Last summer it had been fortune-telling. Zenobia was forever looking into my teacup or inspecting the lines of my palm, then lengthily listing the misfortunes—shipwrecks and pinching shoes and incurable bouts of hiccups—she saw for me in my future.

And ever since she had tired of fortune-telling, it had been clairvoyance. There was nothing—at least for now—that

fascinated Zenobia more than ghosts. And this was unfortunate, because there was nothing I was more afraid of than—

"Well, that's not true," she said.

"Excuse me?"

"You were about to think that there's nothing you're more frightened of than ghosts. The correct nomenclature, by the way, is 'Spirit Presence.' And it's simply not true that there's nothing you're more afraid of. I happen to know you're frightened equally by almost everything."

"I don't think—"

"Seagulls!"

"Yes, but only when they're swooping. Or when they look as if they might swoop."

"Hard-boiled eggs!"

I shuddered. "Too much like eyes."

"Snakes." She was counting on her fingers now. "Music boxes. Gloves without hands in them. Should I continue?"

"I think you've made your point."

Zenobia opened her book, drew out the raven's feather she used for a bookmark, and, holding it between her teeth, began to read.

I can't read other people's thoughts, but I knew Zenobia well enough to know what she was thinking: that in the new house she might finally encounter a Spirit Presence.

I watched Zenobia while she read. She was too absorbed in her book to notice how I shivered.

At the next station, the door to our compartment opened and two girls came in. One tall, one small, and both in school uniform. The small one took the seat by Father, and the tall one, before I could stop her, sat squarely on Zenobia. Almost immediately, she sprang up again. Her face was pale and her teeth chattered. She folded her arms tightly around herself.

"What's the matter this time, Cecilia?" Annoyance flickered over the small girl's face.

"The cold," said Cecilia. "Didn't you feel it?"

"I didn't feel anything."

Cecilia stared at the place where Zenobia sat. "I felt it," she said. "I felt it even in my teeth and in my hair. I've never felt so cold."

"Well, I don't know what you're talking about."

Cecilia turned about the carriage. "There must be a draft," she concluded. And she sat on her case on the floor.

Zenobia smiled and went on reading her book.

"How long to go?" I asked Zenobia when the small girl and the tall girl had left. She snapped open the silver watch. "Fifty-three minutes," she said, "if we're running on time."

She went back to her book. I went back to the fogged window.

The thought that the train would soon stop—that I would have to get off at a strange station, go to a strange house, and start to call it home—was like something sharp stuck in my throat that I couldn't swallow away. Then again, perhaps things might be different in the new house. Maybe Father would talk to me at breakfast and dinner, or leave the door to his study open so I could come and stand by him while he worked, or even invite me to accompany him on his afternoon walks. Maybe he would stop remembering Mother was gone and start remembering I was still there.

When the train pulled away from Witheringe Green, Father, Zenobia, and I were the only figures on the platform. If anyone else had gotten off the train, they had quickly been lost in the thickening fog.

2
Mrs. Purswell

ll I could see outside the car window was fog. I stared
in front of me instead, at the back of Father's head
and the head of the driver who had met us at the
station house.

"Dr. Murmur?" he had asked, appearing out of the fog. "For
Witheringe House?"

"That's right," said Father.

"Mrs. Purswell sent me," said the man, and Father nodded.
It seemed he knew who Mrs. Purswell was.

The man drove us out of the station and past the village of
Witheringe Green, though I couldn't see it through the grayness.
We started up a hill so steep, it was almost vertical. Halfway up,
the driver stopped.

"Witheringe House," he said. "Or the gates, anyhow. The
rest of the way is too steep for the car."

He walked ahead carrying a lamp so we could see in front of ourselves. I strained to catch sight of the new house. But apart from the skeleton shapes of trees and a glinting that might have come from the glass of a window, I saw nothing but fog.

As I came closer, I started to make out the outline of the house. It was stone, the same gray color as the fog, and its roof was turreted and shingled. It looked like it had stood empty a long time.

On the crumbling front step of the new house stood a sharp-faced, sharp-eyed woman. A worn crocodile-skin bag sat at her feet.

"Mrs. Purswell," said Father. "I hope you haven't been waiting long."

"I've just arrived, sir," she said.

"Just arrived?" Zenobia's voice came close in my ear. "She looks like she's been standing there a hundred years, exposed to all the elements."

"She does look," I admitted, "a little weather-beaten."

"She looks like one of those gargoyles"—Zenobia pointed up—"has crawled down from the roof."

I didn't look where Zenobia pointed. Gargoyles, with their bulging eyes, frighten me.

"Of course they do," muttered Zenobia. At the same time, Father said, "Mrs. Purswell, this is my daughter, Elizabeth."

Mrs. Purswell nodded at me. Her eyes passed over the place where Zenobia stood.

"I've engaged Mrs. Purswell as our housekeeper once more," Father said. He spoke to me, not Mrs. Purswell, who had plucked a brass key from the key ring rattling at her hip and disappeared through the door into the greeny-dark insides of Witheringe House. Father followed her, and Zenobia and I went next, feeling small under the high ceiling of the front hall. The hall opened onto a large room. At one end of it a broad staircase went up three levels. Half-dead palm trees in porcelain pots drooped on either side of the stairs. At the other end a dusty tapestry hung from the ceiling. Its fringed edge drooped onto the floor. Mrs. Purswell yanked the curtains open, and light spilled thinly in.

"Oh!" Zenobia clasped her hands together. "It's like a solemn congregation of Spirits!"

She was talking, I guessed, about the furniture veiled with white dust sheets. But Mrs. Purswell, finished with the curtains, was soon whipping off the sheets and folding them into neat squares. And then the shrouded shapes weren't spirits at all. Just furniture. But strange furniture. Dressers and sideboards and winged armchairs that looked like the serious grandparents of the furniture Mother had chosen for our house in the city.

"Some people"—Zenobia eyed Mrs. Purswell—"have no regard for atmosphere."

I said nothing. Personally, I hoped the armchair-ghosts and sideboard-ghosts were the only spirits haunting Witheringe House.

Zenobia's scornful eyes were on me now. "Well, I hope you're wrong," she said. "And there's only one way to find out."

She took her watch from the folds of her dress and buffed it with her sleeve. Then, pretending to be interested in the needle-point pattern of a cushion Mrs. Purswell had just plumped, she began to swing the watch on its chain. It made slow silver circles in the gloom. This was from *The World Beyond* by Famed and Celebrated Clairvoyant Madame Lucent, Chapter Three: "How to Locate the Mysterious Presences at Work Around You, in Five Simple Steps."

Step One: To determine if a Spirit is Present in your Home or Surrounds, first Ostentatiously display something Shiny. Spirits, like Magpies, are attracted by things that Glint or Sparkle. Hold your Shiny Thing so it is easily visible and as you do so pay Close Attention to any Changes in the Atmosphere about you. Does a Door Creak? Do you Feel a sudden Chill? Does the mist of Spirit Breath appear on the Surface of your Shiny Thing?

Zenobia stilled the watch's chain and brought its ticking face closer to her own. She inspected it carefully.

"Well?" I asked.

"I think," she said, "there was a faint misting on the watch case. But it's gone now."

Mrs. Purswell was talking with Father. "I shall give the house a good airing," she was saying, "and then I shall make up the bedrooms. I expect you'll take the large bedroom closest to the library, Dr. Murmur?"

"Very good," said Father.

"And for Miss Elizabeth . . ." She looked me up and down. It was a look that made me want to stand up straighter. I pushed my shoulders down and uncurled my spine. "The only room suited to a child"—she spoke over my head—"is the nursery."

I felt a creeping red come over my face. I was definitely too old for the nursery.

"Not the nursery," said Father firmly. "In fact, Mrs. Purswell, it won't be necessary for you to open the East Wing at all. Nor for you to poke around in it, Elizabeth."

I nodded.

"We will hardly need so much space," Father went on. "After all, we are only two."

"Three," said Zenobia. "We are three." And she unloosed a button from her cuff and let it fall to the carpet.

*Step Two: Find a Spare Button in your Sewing Box
or Unloose one from About your Person. Drop it to the
floor and let it Remain There for fifteen minutes at a
Minimum. If, on your return, it has Disappeared, it has
likely been taken by a Spirit. Spirits are forever losing
their Buttons and will therefore take any that they see
Unattended.*

Mrs. Purswell looked at me, thoughtfully. "The blue guest bedroom, then, sir?" she said at last.

"The blue guest bedroom," said Father, "will do very well."

The first dinner in the new house was mostly silent. Father sat at one end of the long polished table. Zenobia and I sat at the other. The dining room was dark and shadowy in its corners. From one of these corners, Mrs. Purswell materialized. Her apron was very white against the darkness.

"I expect"—she ladled soup into bowls—"you'll want something light after your journey."

The soup was pale green. An exploratory stirring revealed weedy leaves floating through it. I brought a spoonful to my mouth, but before I could taste it, Zenobia cleared her throat.

"Father," I said. And again, when he made no sign he had heard me, "Father!"

His voice came down the table, faint and irritated. "Yes?"

I angled my head at the place beside me. He looked, for a second, tired. Then he said, "Very well, Elizabeth. Mrs. Purswell?"

The shadows in the corner shifted and thickened, and Mrs. Purswell stepped out of them again. "I hope it's not too much trouble," said Father, "but we need an extra setting by Elizabeth. Zenobia has joined us for dinner."

"Of course, sir." Mrs. Purswell laid another bowl and silverware beside me. I liked her better for the incurious way she accepted Zenobia's presence.

Zenobia took up her spoon. She admired her reflection, first convex, then concave, on its surface. Then she bit down on it hard. "Nice," she said. "Real silver." She pressed the bowl of the spoon into the deep hollow of her eye socket and grinned. "The kind they lay on dead men's eyes."

"That's not really dinner-table conversation," I told her, just like Mother used to tell Father in the old house whenever he talked too long about photosynthesis.

Zenobia looked at me. She looked down the table at Father, whose eyes never lifted from his soup bowl. She looked at me again. "It's the only conversation, in case you hadn't noticed," she said. "You may as well not be here"—she jerked the spoon in Father's direction—"as far as he's concerned."

My stomach twisted. I didn't want Zenobia's words to be true.

"You're wrong," I said, and I searched about for something to say to Father.

I raised myself up in my chair and made my voice very loud. "Do you find the house much changed, Father?"

Father addressed his reply to his soup. "It is just as it was. Perhaps a little dustier."

"It must hold a lot of memories for you," I prompted.

He looked up, spoon poised.

"The house—" My voice cracked. "The house must be full of memories. From when you were a child."

"Ah," he said, and he steered another weedy spoonful under his moustache.

"I suppose," I went on, changing tack, "you'll start your work tomorrow."

At the museum Father had been head of the Botanic Department. His resignation and his return to Witheringe Green would allow him to begin work on a new project: an improved system for the classification of native ferns and wildflowers. The old system, in his opinion, had room for improvement.

"I expect to begin fieldwork shortly," he said.

After this there was only the sound of our spoons sloshing through soup and clinking on the bottoms of our bowls.

Zenobia put her elbows on the table. "The button is gone," she said.

A gust of wind blew the chandelier above us back and forth. Zenobia's face went bright and then shadowed and then bright again with the swaying light.

"I've checked the cobwebs as well," she said. "It wasn't hard. Witheringe House is abundant with cobwebs."

Step Three: If your house is Inhabited by Spiders, observe their Cobwebs closely. A Spider will usually make its Gossamer Web by weaving in a Clockwise Direction. But Spiders are creatures Sensitive to the Presence of Spirits, and if a Spirit is nearby, a Spider will weave its Web Widdershins.

"And are they?" I asked.

"Widdershins," she said. "Definitely widdershins."

Zenobia took out her watch, opened its case, and laid it flat on the table. It was two minutes to eight. She watched its second hand tick twice around its face. Then she took up her salad fork, tested the tines on her finger, and held it in the air.

Of course. Step Four.

Step Four: With a Tuning Fork if you are able to Procure One, or a Salad Fork if you are not, Test for Spirit Vibrations in the Air at the time when the clock Strikes

the Hour. The small spaces in time between one Hour
and Another are the times when the veil that divides our
Waking World from the World of the Spirits is at its most
Permeable: the closer to Midnight the Hour, the thinner the
Veil between Worlds.

Zenobia's watch showed eight o'clock exactly. The chiming of a clock in another room started. The fork in Zenobia's hand juddered, and she dropped it on the table.

The fork on the mahogany roused Father. "Are you feeling all right, Elizabeth?"

"Fine," I replied. But this was a lie. I was far from fine. In the old house, Zenobia had never gotten as far as Step Four. And this meant she had never progressed to Step Five. And Step Five didn't bear thinking about.

Step Five: If, having carried out these first Four Steps, you
are Satisfied that you have Indeed Located a Mysterious
Presence at work around you, it is Time to continue to the
Fifth and Most Crucial Step in the process. For further
information, Read On to the next chapter: Communing with
the Spirit World (The Keys to Holding a Successful Séance).

Would Zenobia really hold a séance?

"*We* certainly will," she told me. "Tonight."

"You've gone quite pale," said Father. "I expect you're tired. Why don't you go to bed."

It was not a suggestion.

Mrs. Purswell showed me into the blue guest bedroom. Then she nodded and closed the door behind her. Her footsteps faded down the hallway. I looked around. "It's very blue," I said at last.

"Too blue." Zenobia wrinkled her nose. "I detest the color blue."

"You detest all colors," I reminded her.

"Not true. I like black."

"Black's not a color."

"I like certain shades of gray. And I like red. Not bright red, but red the color of old blood. But there are none of those colors here."

"No. Just blue."

The wallpaper was a blue stripe, and the curtains, along with the quilt that matched them, were a slippery sea-blue. The glass shade of the lamp was the blue color of a medicine bottle, and it gave a sick glow to everything it lit. Even the carpet was covered with faded blue flowers.

Zenobia put her hands to her head. "Do you think, Elizabeth, a person can be allergic to the color blue?"

"Perhaps not allergic, exactly."

Zenobia sighed dramatically. "The sooner we put out the light, the better," she said.

"Will it be held in the dark, then?" My voice wobbled.

"Of course it will be held in the dark. It's a séance."

My heart wobbled.

According to Father there were no such things as ghosts.

I took a long time washing and dressing for bed.

There were old perfume bottles and tonic bottles—relics from past guests, I imagined—scattered around the washbasin. I picked these up one by one. I put my nose to them or inspected the long-calcified powders they contained.

According to Father, ghosts were the products of hysterical imaginations.

I washed my neck and behind my ears. I unwound my hair from its two braids and raked through it with my fingers.

According to Father, Zenobia was the product of my hysterical imagination.

And yet I could hear her behind me. Turning the pages of her book.

"Now, Madame Lucent tells us," she read aloud:

"A séance is the meeting point between Our World and the World Beyond. A Crossroads at which we can Command the Spirits and be Commanded by them!

"And—ooh!—this is interesting, Elizabeth. Listen."

Friends, when you Conduct a Séance, Expect only the Unexpected! Perhaps your Spirit is in Want of no more than Polite Conversation on a Topic such as the Weather. Perhaps your Spirit will make the Walls about You drip with Blood!

"I wonder what sort of a Spirit ours will be. If it does prove to be the blood-dripping kind—"

"Don't, Zenobia!"

"I was only going to say it might improve the wallpaper."

I splashed my face with water. In the dust-spotted mirror I saw that I looked scared, so I tried to make myself look brave.

When I turned from my reflection, I saw that Zenobia had laid the necessary equipment on the carpet. A stubby candle in its holder. A matchbook. A length of twine. A silver ring. And the Ouija board, made from thin balsa wood and printed with numbers and the letters of the alphabet. On the board's right side was marked the word "Yes" and on its left side, "No."

"Could you turn out the light, Elizabeth?" Zenobia said, and she struck a match on the side of the matchbook.

"Couldn't we—"

"Couldn't we what?"

"Couldn't we keep the light on?"

"If we must," she said. She cupped the candle so the flame

would take, and she shook the match down to a thin ribbon of smoke.

I sank to the carpet. I bunched my nightgown in my hands so tightly my fingers went white.

Zenobia smiled at me through the candle flame. Then she threaded the silver ring onto the length of twine. She held it, with the ring swaying in the air above the wooden board.

"Let us begin," she said.

3
The Séance

Here." Zenobia thrust the ring at me and flung herself across the bed's blue quilt, face-first among the pillows. When she spoke, her voice was muffled. "I don't understand!"

"I can't hear you very well."

She lifted her head. "I said, I don't understand. We followed Madame Lucent's instructions exactly."

It was true, we had. We'd sat cross-legged on the floor with the index and middle fingers of our left hands pressed to opposite corners of the board. We'd asked all the suggested questions in the recommended order.

O Spirit, what Moves you to Seek Beyond the Veil?
O Spirit, why are you Restless?
O Spirit, tell us of your Troubles!

And all we got—

"All we got were these!" Zenobia waved her hand at the letters I had written with shaking hand on a piece of paper. "They don't even make sense!"

"I'm sure we can arrange them to spell out something," I soothed. "Didn't Madame Lucent say we shouldn't expect any message from the World Beyond to be straightforward?"

"You can stop pretending you're not secretly pleased," she snapped. "You didn't want the séance to work in the first place." She let her head fall into the pillows again.

And then the room went cold, and I went cold with it. Zenobia jerked up. Her eyes were sharp with excitement. The twine in my hand started to spin. The silver ring moved from letter to letter like it was being pulled by an invisible hand.

T-C-K-I-K-N-G-O-E

I wanted to drop the twine, but my fingers were locked around it.

N-L-P-A-E-E-S-D

Finally, the twine slowed and stilled. The cold subsided, but the hairs on my arms and on my neck still stood straight up.

Zenobia, as close to smiling as I had ever seen her, crouched beside me. "I knew it," she said. "I knew there was a Spirit Presence at work. Now, what did it say?"

I shook my head. "It moved so quickly, I couldn't write the letters down."

"But what were they? Try to remember."

"There was a G. I think a K. More than one E."

My eye caught the flicking corner of the blue curtain. I gave the twine to Zenobia and went to the window.

"More than one E," said Zenobia, "and what else? What other letters? What are you doing?"

"I think I've found the Spirit Presence," I told her, and I showed her the wide-open window. Another gust of wind blew in and once more the room went cold and the ring spun in hectic circles above the Ouija board.

Zenobia let the twine drop from her hands. She looked sad. And then she looked angry.

The candle guttered and blew out.

The bulb in the blue lampshade splintered.

The room went dark.

"Was that necessary?" I asked.

"All that vile blueness was giving me a headache," she said.

"But how will I explain the broken lamp to Mrs. Purswell?"

"I wish you would be quiet, Elizabeth. I find myself overcome with exhaustion. I want only to sleep."

In darkness, I groped my way from the window to the bed. The mattress was hard and narrow. I slept with Zenobia's icy body pressed close to mine and the wind—nothing more than the wind—troubling the windowpane.

When I pushed back the curtain in the morning (quietly, because Zenobia was still sleeping), I saw the fog had thinned. A silvery rain fell instead. The window of the blue guest bedroom, I saw now, looked out onto a ruined garden that struggled up the steep slope on which Witheringe House was built. It was dead, except for the places where it was overgrown with weeds. I spied a sundial, half-eaten by ivy, and a dark tangle of hedge that I realized, after I squinted at it some more, was supposed to be a maze. At the center of the maze grew a tall tree. The tree had a dry, dead look. Its branches made sinister shapes against the gloomy sky, and I quickly turned my gaze away to a falling-down shed perched at the peak of the slope. It looked as if it had been built at the edge of the world.

When at last I came away from the window, Zenobia was awake and sitting propped against a pile of pillows. Her book was open to Chapter Six. I saw the title over her shoulder: "Recalcitrant Spirits, Some Strategies."

Father was not in the dining room. A plate with crumbs and eggshells and a crumpled napkin sat on the table before his empty chair. I swallowed away my disappointment. I liked Father's company at the breakfast table. Even if we didn't speak, I liked to hear the rustle of his newspaper and the scrape of his knife against his toast.

"Ten minutes to eight," said Zenobia, "and already done with breakfast."

"It makes sense." I defended him. "He did say he wanted to get an early start on his fieldwork." I turned to take my seat and collided, instead, with the stiff bodice of Mrs. Purswell's serge pinafore.

"Good morning, Miss Elizabeth," said Mrs. Purswell as I backed away, stammering apologies.

"It's quite remarkable the way she does that," said Zenobia.

"Does what?" I whispered.

"Just appears. Out of nowhere. The art of the sudden and unsettling entrance is not an easy one to master. Believe me. I've tried."

Mrs. Purswell cleared Father's empty plate and folded his napkin over her arm. She set a place for me and one beside me, without my having to ask, for Zenobia.

"Thank you," I murmured. But my thanks were addressed to thin air, because Mrs. Purswell was gone.

"Remarkable," breathed Zenobia. "Now"—she turned to me—"I've been thinking about last night's séance."

It would've been nice to have finished buttering my toast before the talk came around to séances.

"It was not a success," continued Zenobia.

"Perhaps not." I spread the butter carefully up to the crust and then reached for the marmalade.

"It was presumptuous of me to expect to commune with our Spirit Presence straightaway."

"So you do still think there is a Spirit Presence?" It had been foolish of me to hope the failed séance might spell an end to Zenobia's ghostly quest.

"Yes."

"And you do want to keep looking for it?"

"We will continue to seek it out, yes."

"Oh." I bit down on a toast triangle.

"But I now believe we are dealing with what Madame Lucent terms a Recalcitrant Spirit."

"And what is that, exactly?"

"I'm glad you asked," said Zenobia. She opened her book and began to read.

"Some Spirits like to Reveal themselves Immediately. It is on Account of Spirits such as these that we hear Tales of Rapping and Moaning, Tales of Respectable Elderly Aunts being Possessed by the long-drowned ghosts of Cornish Sailors and uttering Strings of Foul Profanity and calling for Rum to be added to their Tea. But there are Other Spirits—Spirits that are Shy, Unsociable, even Secretive. They are Loath to make contact with our Waking World. But! With care it is Sometimes Possible to draw them out. I myself have—"

"She likes talking about herself, doesn't she?"

"Fine," said Zenobia. "We'll skip that part."

"Other guides to the Spirit World give only the Vaguest Clues to Locating the Shy and Secretive Spirit. They suggest the Seeker hope to be struck by such Vague and Tenebrous Phenomena as a Feeling of Acute Sadness or an Itch at the Nape of the Neck—both things which might indicate the Presence of a Spirit but which might equally indicate the Presence of a Scalp Condition. Fortunately, I Myself have developed a Strategy which has been Praised—"

Maybe Zenobia saw me rolling my eyes, because here she closed the book and said, "Well, in essence Madame Lucent says we are to walk through the house, room to room, carrying with us a single flower—a flower in bud or very early blossom—which will act as a kind of divining rod, alerting us when we are near to the Spirit."

"It's very . . . poetic," I said carefully. "But I don't see how it works."

"Well, this is the clever part," Zenobia said. She went to the sideboard and plucked a bud from an arrangement of roses and ferns. "If, when we enter the room, the flower withers and dies, then we know that the Spirit Presence is near."

"But—"

"It's scientific! It's a known fact that an arrangement of flowers cannot stay alive in a room inhabited by a Spirit Presence. Madame Lucent proves it in this very book—Chapter Nine: 'Eleven and a Half Incontrovertible Proofs for the Existence of Spirits'!"

"Well"—I looked at the roses on the sideboard, blooming and fragrant—"there's no ghost here."

"No Spirit Presence," corrected Zenobia. "Which means we'll have to look elsewhere."

"We will?"

"We will." She looked pointedly at my plate. "As soon as you've finished your toast."

I am not a fast eater, but I was especially slow finishing my last toast triangle. I had even planned to spend some time wiping crumbs and marmalade globules from my plate with my fingers, but as soon as I had taken my last bite, Mrs. Purswell materialized to clear the table, and Zenobia, armed with a creamy rosebud on a long green stem, started for the door.

"The house is a lot cleaner looking," sniffed Zenobia. "That lovely layer of dust has been whisked away. I had been planning on taking some for my dust collection. Still, it retains a pleasant sort of dinginess."

We stood at the place where the entrance hall opened out into the front room, the same room Mrs. Purswell had ushered us into when we arrived yesterday.

"Now," Zenobia said, "I wonder where might be the best place to start. We could begin in there." She pointed at a half-open door that showed a room partly filled with an arrangement of taxidermied animals. "Or there's an intriguingly dark corridor on the second floor that looked promising? But perhaps we should be methodical. Yes." She strode to the foot of the staircase. "We'll go up to the top floor and work our way down." And she led the way up the stairs.

We came to a heavy wooden door and Zenobia stopped. I stopped behind her, feeling fear start to prickle along my scalp and down my spine and wondering why I had followed Zenobia on her ghost hunt.

"It's not a ghost hunt, Elizabeth. It's a search for a Spirit Presence. And I'll tell you why you follow me."

"Oh?"

"You follow me because there is one thing you're frightened of more than ghosts or the black keys on the piano—truly pathetic things to be afraid of, if you ask me."

"It's just that the black keys always sound so much more ominous."

"You're afraid of being ignored. Of being alone."

That's not true, I wanted to say. But it wouldn't have been entirely accurate. So I said instead, "That's not nice."

"Perhaps it isn't," Zenobia replied, and she tested the door with outstretched fingers.

It swung open.

Sometimes I wondered why I was friends with Zenobia.

She walked into the room with her arms straight out in front of her and the flower in her hands.

"Well," she asked over her shoulder, "are you coming?"

I told her I supposed I was.

I took a small step through the door. As soon as I did, there came a sharp, shrieking sound. I covered my face with my hands. I felt the blood beating in my fingers and my heart beating against my ribs.

"A loose floorboard," Zenobia said.

"Oh." I tried the floorboard again with the tip of my shoe. It produced the same shrieking sound. Slowly, stepping around the loose board, I went through the doorway and into a small room with pink walls and a hard-looking sofa covered in pink velvet the color of tongue.

I came up behind Zenobia. "Has the flower—"

"See for yourself," she said.

The bud was closed tight. Its leaves were a fresh pale green and it smelled of springtime. There was no Spirit Presence here.

We went from room to room, and in each one Zenobia held the flower out in front of her. In each room the petals stayed white and fresh. And as room after room proved itself free from ghosts, I began to feel easier.

I started to enjoy exploring my new house. In the ballroom, I turned my face up to see my reflection in the mirrored ceiling. In the games room, I ran my palms over the green felt of the billiards table. I found, in some rooms, secret doors, covered over to look like part of the wallpaper, to linen cupboards or dumbwaiters.

We came through a narrow corridor to the door of a large room with a domed ceiling and walls lined with bookshelves.

Zenobia started forward but I caught her sleeve and tugged her back.

"This is the library," I whispered. "Father could be at work. We don't want to disturb him."

Zenobia stuck her neck around the door. "We won't disturb him," she said. "He's not here."

"Are you sure?" I curled my fingers around the doorframe.

"Quite sure." She beckoned me across the library to the window and pointed down to the garden, where Father was walking. He looked, from the third-floor window, very small.

"He must be collecting specimens," I said at last.

"It doesn't look like he's collecting anything," said Zenobia. "See the way his hands are jammed into his jacket pockets."

"But he's looking for specimens, at least."

"Shouldn't he be looking at the ground, then? Looking for flowers and ferns and not staring off into the distance like that?"

"In any case," I said firmly, "a refreshing walk will be doing him good."

I moved away from the window and looked about the library, breathing in the old-book smell that filled the air. In one corner was a stack of gramophone records. Near the top, one record stuck out: *The Magic Flute*. I eased it out of the pile and hid it carefully under the carpet.

The library shelves were only half-filled. Some books were still in boxes and others were piled on the floor. I read the titles on their spines.

> *Ascomycota: From Spore to Stem*
> *Linnaean Taxonomy: A Modern Approach*
> *Cactaceae Considered*
> *Adventures with Anemones*

I picked up one book, a heavy brown one with the title etched in green. *The Plant Kingdom* by Dr. Henry Murmur. This was Father's first book, though he must have written hundreds by now. I flipped it open. Its pages were filled with small black type interrupted now and again by color plates depicting plants. They were linked with lines and arrows like the branches of a family tree, showing how this dandelion was related to that nettle and so on.

"What's that?" Zenobia looked over my shoulder.

"It's Father's book," I said.

"I thought it must be," she said, "on account of it looking impossibly dull."

"Perhaps it is," I said. "I've never read it. But it's funny—"

I stopped.

"What's funny?"

"Only that when I was young, Father used to read to me from his book. But he didn't read the words written on the page. He made it into a story, instead. The story of the Plant Kingdom. It was a real place with a King and a Queen, and it was filled with strange plant-people with roots instead of feet. The Queen had rose-petal hair and the King had branches instead of hands. Do you remember?"

It was hard to believe, now, that Father had ever told such stories, and yet he had. Some nights he had stayed up until midnight with me, telling me of adventures in the Plant Kingdom.

"I remember the story was incredibly boring," said Zenobia, "all sunshine and flowers and talking hedgerows. But I liked the Plant King, with his tiny twisted eyes, like knots in wood, his beard of slithering worms, and his mouth full of black beetles."

I shuddered. I had never liked the Plant King.

"It wasn't boring at all. It was—not that I'd expect you to understand—it was nice. Really nice. It used to be my favorite thing, Father reading to me from *The Plant Kingdom* at bedtime."

I flipped to the back of the book, then to the front. My eye caught on the first page. "I didn't know it had a dedication. *To dearest Tourmaline*, it says."

Zenobia sucked her breath in slowly. "Elizabeth—"

"Tourmaline. Tourmaline. That's not Mother's name. I wonder who Tourmaline could be . . ."

"Elizabeth!"

Zenobia grabbed me by both arms and spun me around to see Father standing in the doorway. The shoulders of his black jacket were beaded with raindrops. His face was clouded. His voice, when he spoke, was dark.

"Who were you talking with just now, Elizabeth?"

He stood, tall, over me. His shadow, even taller, spread across the carpet.

I looked at Zenobia, guilty for what I was about to say.

"Nobody."

"I see," said Father. At the same time, the open book snapped shut on my fingers, and I bit down hard on the inside of my cheek to stop myself from crying out.

"I'm nobody now, am I?" hissed Zenobia.

I would need to take extra care to be nice to her later. Maybe if I found Father's *Complete Works of Poe* and listened to her recite from her favorite poem, "The Raven," she might forgive me.

Father wriggled his arms out of his coat and laid it over the back of his chair. "I won't join you for lunch," he said, and he sat down at his desk. "Ask Mrs. Purswell to send me up a tray."

"Yes, Father."

He turned in his chair so that his back was toward me. "You are excused."

I edged out the door and into the hallway. I caught up with Zenobia, who had already stormed away in a huff. We were halfway down the stairs before I realized I still held the book in my hands.

That evening, I sat on the guest bedroom's worn blue carpet and watched Zenobia launch into her third recitation of "The Raven." I looked down at the blue flowers—tulips, I thought they were—covering the carpet whenever the poem grew too scary. "The Raven" is a poem about a man who receives a midnight visit from a hellish, talking raven, so I spent a lot of time looking at the blue carpet-tulips.

Zenobia's voice grew louder and the candle flickered lower with each stanza she recited.

"'Be that word our sign of parting, bird or fiend!'
I shrieked, upstarting—"

And she did shriek and she upstarted as well, springing up onto the washbasin.

"'Get thee back into the tempest and the Night's Plutonian shore!

Leave no black plume as a token of that lie thy soul hath spoken!

Leave my loneliness unbroken!—quit the bust above my door!'"

For this last line, she stopped to take hold of a perfume bottle, and she hurled the bottle over my head and against the wall. It shattered, leaving an oily stain on the blue paper. And she yelled:

" 'Take thy beak from out of my heart, and take thy form from off my door!'"

Then she crouched low in the sink, one heel sinking into a cake of soap. She held her black skirt out around her to look like a pair of black wings and she made her voice into something like a croak.

"Quoth the raven, 'Nevermore.'"

"Very . . . nice," I said, clapping for a polite amount of time.

Zenobia stepped out of the sink, wiped the soap off her shoe, and made a sweeping bow. "I'm afraid that concludes my recitation," she said. "I'm too exhausted to perform further." And she lay stretched out on the carpet. "I think I'll spend some time reading Mr. Poe before bed."

She brought the candle close to her. I reached, in the absence of anything else to read, for *The Plant Kingdom* by Dr. Henry Murmur. I sat by Zenobia in the small pool of candlelight and tried to pay attention to what Father had written, sounding out the words (genus, stamen, anther, anemophily—I thought anemophily sounded particularly nice) that I hadn't heard before. But soon my eyes were following the words down the page without my mind keeping up, and I had to go back to the top and start again. And again. And then again. Each time I started over, my eyes grew heavier. At last they fell closed.

I crawled into bed half-asleep. When I woke it was dark and Zenobia lay breathing heavily beside me. I sat up, listening to the creakings and murmurings of the house and the murky chiming of the clocks, different clocks in different rooms and none of them quite keeping time with the others. Quarter after eleven. Half-past eleven. Quarter to midnight and I was still lying awake. With small, quiet movements, I lit the candle and took my book from the table by the bed. It had put me to sleep once earlier and I hoped it would have the same effect now.

It almost did.

When the clock struck twelve, I had yawned my way three pages into a chapter on *Asteraceae Taraxacum*, the dandelion genus. My eyes felt gluey. My fingers fumbled clumsily over the pages.

But the next page I turned to was not like the ones that had come before it. It was filled with looping green letters that unfurled across the paper like a vine growing over a trellis. I wondered if my tired eyes were tricking me. I moved the page closer to the candle. But the letters stayed the same. And now I could see that they spelled out a story.

This tale begins in the way these tales often do. With a Kingdom. One full of green and growing things. And a King, who had branches instead of hands, and a Queen with rose-petal hair. The King and Queen were good and just, and they ruled their kingdom well. But they were not happy. They could never be happy. For they had no child.

Until one day, a small miracle. The Queen sat on her throne. The Head Gardener churned through the soil on his roots toward her, unrolling a long petition as he did.

"The Union of Roses and Carnations," said the Head Gardener, "requests permission to extend the northern perimeters of their flower beds."

"Approved," said the Queen.

"The caterpillars," continued the Gardener, "request an amnesty from predatory avian parties during the larval season."

But the Queen didn't reply. Instead, she brought one celery-green hand very close to her face. Then she spread her leafy palm wide and held it out to the Gardener.

"Look at this," she said. "It's like—"

"Yes," said the Gardener. "It's very like—"

It was very like a cocoon. Gossamer-soft. And with something growing inside it.

The cocoon was placed under a lamp in the nursery to keep it warm day and night. Each day it grew until one day it tore and split, and out tumbled a tiny boy with grassy hair and a healthy set of roots.

And the King and Queen were happy at last.

Here the page ended and the story ended with it. The next pages showed only the small black print and the same precise diagrams that had come before it.

In the morning, after a fitful sleep, I opened the book to the chapter on *Asteraceae Taraxacum*. The page with the green letters wasn't there. I went to the start of the book and worked my way to the end. Nothing.

I wondered if I had dreamed it, in one of those dreams that feel as clear and real as life when you are in them.

I looked down at the book in my lap and frowned.

Yes, it must have been one of those dreams.

4

The East Wing

I slid my empty teacup across the table to where Zenobia sat with her chin in her hands.

"Don't you want to read the leaves?" I prompted.

"You know I've given up fortune-telling," she said.

"But some terrible fate might await me," I coaxed. "I might get attacked by a—by a cat! A larger-than-normal cat! With sharp teeth and claws!"

Zenobia lifted an eyebrow.

"Don't look at me like that," I said. "You know you're much better at thinking up terrible misfortunes than I am."

But she pushed the cup away. "Not today," she said.

We had been four long, rainy days at Witheringe House, and Zenobia was still no closer to finding any kind of Spirit Presence. As each day passed, free from ghosts or messages from Beyond the Veil, I felt my nerves start to ease. But Zenobia slid into a melancholy. Usually she enjoyed her melancholies, but this one was, even by her standards, extreme. And as much as I'd hoped she wouldn't find a ghost, it made me sad to see her sadness.

That afternoon I found a copy of *Hamlet* in the library. I took it to the seat by the rain-slicked window where Zenobia sat, and I pressed it into her hands. "Wouldn't you like to read it?" I asked. "I've marked all the gruesome parts."

"Maybe later," she said.

I climbed onto the window seat beside her. "You know, there's a dead spider behind one of the curtains in the music room," I said. "Mrs. Purswell must have missed it when she dusted." Zenobia had always loved performing elaborate funerals for dead insects. She laid them out on her black silk handkerchief and deliberated over whether to read from Edward Young's "Night Thoughts" (*Lovely in death the beauteous ruin lay)* or "The Grave" by Robert Blair (*Dull grave! Thou spoil'st the dance of youthful blood*) for the eulogy. She almost always chose the Blair. His meter, she said, was more thrilling.

"It's starting to shrivel up," I said. "You know you love that shrivelly shape spiders get after they've been dead a day or two."

"I know what you're trying to do, Elizabeth." She raised her head. "And I appreciate it, really. But you won't cheer me. Nothing can cheer me now."

"It can't be as bad as all that," I said, and I wrapped my fingers through hers.

"But it *is* as bad as all that. I've done everything Madame Lucent instructed me to do and—nothing. We've searched every room in the West Wing with no sign of—"

She dropped my hand.

"Every room in the West Wing," she said again. "In the West Wing."

"Are you feeling all right, Zenobia?"

"Oh, I'm better than all right—and do you know why?"

I shook my head.

"Because a thought has just struck me, Elizabeth! We've searched *only* the West Wing—we haven't explored the East Wing at all!"

My stomach shrank.

Zenobia sprang down from the seat and pulled me toward the door.

"But we can't go in the East Wing," I said. "We're not allowed to. Father said."

"Your father won't notice if you go into the East Wing."

"How can you be so sure?"

"Your father would hardly notice if you grew twelve feet tall, started speaking Mandarin, and set your hair on fire!"

And she marched off down the dark corridor. I stayed, try-ing to convince myself that Zenobia was wrong. But I couldn't manage it. Ever since Mother had left, I wondered if Father noticed me at all.

"Wait for me," I called, and I followed Zenobia into the gloom.

Zenobia stood in the front room. In one hand she held a rose, fresh-plucked from the arrangement in the dining room, and in the other, *The World Beyond* by Madame Lucent.

"I'm quite sure that we'll find our Spirit Presence in the East Wing, Elizabeth," she said. "I have a sense for these things." She squinted around the room. "Only, where do you suppose the East Wing is, exactly?"

"I don't know," I said. I hovered at the bottom step of the staircase, arms curled tight around the banister. "I only know I'm strictly forbidden to enter it."

"Well, help me look, would you?"

I checked the books on the shelves.

"After all, any one of them might prove to be the handle to a hidden doorway," Zenobia told me.

Zenobia knocked on all the walls, in case there was an entryway hidden behind one of the panels. She did find a door half-hidden behind a large dresser.

"There's nothing behind it," she reported. "Just an empty room with lots of dead moths on the floor. I took some lovely moth dust for my collection"—she showed me the powdery moth-wing residue on her outstretched finger—"but we're no closer to finding the East Wing."

"Perhaps," I said, "we're not supposed to find the East Wing today. Perhaps it's a sign."

"Of course!" she said. "What an uncharacteristically apposite idea, Elizabeth!"

"Oh?"

"If the East Wing is inhabited by a Spirit Presence—and I think we both know that it is—then surely the Spirit will manifest some kind of sign to guide us in its direction."

"I don't think that's what I meant."

"Here." She pushed the rose into my hands and opened the book. "Chapter Four," she muttered, "'Signs and Portents.' It's merely a matter of finding the correct invocation."

Her eyes ran down the page.

"Ah! Here it is!" She cleared her throat. When she next spoke, her voice was deep and filled the room from floor to ceiling. "'O Spirit!'" she intoned. "'Guide us down the Shadowed Path that leads to Your Presence!'"

"What now?" I asked when the echoing of Zenobia's words had thinned and stopped.

"Now we wait."

"Wait for what, exactly?"

"A sign, Elizabeth, a sign. The sudden cracking of a

windowpane or mirror. The appearance of a large black bird—crow, raven, the exact species doesn't matter. Or—"

I shivered as the air turned cold and watery. "Or a chill wind?" I asked.

Zenobia thought. "Yes," she said. "It's unoriginal, certainly, but a chill wind could indeed be a sign."

The wind whipped up, rustling the curtains and swelling the tapestry on the far wall. And there, behind the billowing tapestry, was the beginning of a staircase.

"Come," Zenobia said, pulling back the tapestry, "The Spirit World awaits."

I stood in front of the tapestry. My hands were shaking. They shook so hard, they shivered the petals of the rose.

Zenobia crouched and stuck her head beneath the tapestry's fringe. "It's very gloomy back here," she reported, "which is extremely promising."

"You're interested in the tapestry, Miss Elizabeth?"

I straightened up and turned around. Mrs. Purswell stood behind me. She held a flat wooden paddle for beating the dust from curtains and carpets.

Zenobia stepped out from under the tapestry and regarded Mrs. Purswell admiringly. "One day, Elizabeth, you'll have to ask her how she does that. She's elevated lurking to an art."

Mrs. Purswell flicked the wooden paddle briskly against her skirt. She was waiting for my answer.

"Well, it's interesting, isn't it?" I stepped back as if to admire the scene it depicted: a group of people in medieval dress. Two men were standing under tree branches. And a woman, playing a pear-shaped instrument, was sitting in a field of embroidered wildflowers.

"Perhaps it is," said Mrs. Purswell. She looked at me carefully. "Mind you don't find it too interesting." And she left, flicking her paddle as she went.

Zenobia pushed the tapestry aside so I could climb under it, too, and when I paused with my foot hovering over the bottom step, she whispered, "*Will* you come on, Elizabeth?"

And just like that we were in the East Wing.

The staircase was steep and narrow, and we had been climbing it a long, long time when it finally opened out into a corridor.

A very dark corridor. It might also have been very long but it was too dark to see where it ended. Or if it ended at all.

I blinked into the darkness until I could see that it was lined with paintings: portraits of people with thin, serious faces and old-fashioned clothes.

"You're dawdling, Elizabeth," Zenobia called over her shoulder, "and I'm quite sure you're doing it on purpose."

"I was just looking at the portraits. I guess they must be of my family."

Zenobia turned to a portrait of a woman in a tall silvery wig. She touched her fingers to the painting's dusty frame. "Perhaps one of these portraits," she said, "shows our Spirit Presence—while they still walked among the World of the Living, I mean."

Then she tapped the dust from her fingertips into her pocket. "For my collection," she said.

I hurried past a mean-eyed man—I hoped he wasn't the Spirit Presence—and then past a lady who held a green feather quill in her hand.

After the lady with the quill, the corridor came to an end.

We stood before a door made of wood so dark it was almost black. Zenobia took the doorknob in her hand, swung the door open, and went inside. I went in behind her.

Inside it was even darker than it was in the corridor. The air was thick and smelled of mouse. Even worse, when I took a step a sudden skittering started under my feet. And the room filled with eerie music, an out-of-tune violin playing a slow, mournful song.

My greatest fear. Zenobia's greatest wish. This, then, was the Spirit Presence. And while it had always been my plan that if Zenobia did make contact with the World Beyond, I would run as far as I could in the opposite direction, I found my feet stuck to the floor and my limbs unwilling to move.

"O Spirit!" Zenobia greeted the Spirit Presence ecstatically. "You have Lifted the Veil to our Waking World."

The music kept on. Each note felt like a cold finger running down my neck.

"O Spirit, we are Eager to receive you!" Zenobia's voice rose and cracked.

And then my feet came unstuck and the nerves in my arms and legs began working once more, and I knew I wanted to be far away. As far away from this room, from this whole wretched house, as I could possibly be.

I turned to go outside, to run down the hall and down the stairs. But it was too dark to see properly and my outstretched hands found heavy curtains instead of the wooden door.

I flung the curtains open and light came in.

"A toy," said Zenobia with disdain. She held a clockwork kitten between two fingers. It had a blue ribbon around its neck, a violin tucked under its chin, and a bow held in one jerking paw. The notes it played grew slower and slurred together as it wound down.

With the curtains open we could see we were standing in a nursery. Two bare cots were pushed up against one wall. I sat on the one nearest me. I pushed my palms into the thin mattress and waited for my heart, swollen with fear, to return to its normal size.

Zenobia stood in the middle of the room with the flower held out in front of her.

I looked around the nursery. A shelf held a dusty collection of books. *Struwwelpeter. The Yellow Fairy Book.* A ball, sewn from bright scraps of fabric, lay on the floor. A rocking horse rocked slowly in a corner. A murky mirror hung crooked on one wall. I caught myself in it. My reflection was shifting and rippled, more like the reflection you would find on the surface of a pond than a mirror's glass.

"I am certain there is a Presence here, in this very room," announced Zenobia. "Do you not feel it, too? Do you not feel a *frisson*?"

"I'd need to know what a *frisson* was before I could know if I felt one or not," I said.

"It's a delightful shiver of mystery and terror and pleasure all combined."

"I do feel a shiver, though I wouldn't say it was a *frisson*. I'm inclined to put it down to the wallpaper."

Nursery wallpaper usually shows smiling suns peeking from behind clouds, or characters from Mother Goose, or sprays of soft pink roses growing over white lattice.

This wallpaper was quite different. It was vivid green and it showed a garden, but a strange garden. Every inch of the paper crawled with vines and tendrils. The wallpaper's plants grew in colors and shapes and sizes I had never known plants to grow in before. Their leaves were frog-skin green and rippled with veins. Their flowers were bright as gems. They grew in star shapes and diamond shapes and cornet shapes—any shape other than flower shape.

A twisted tree, sprouting dark spiky leaves, took up most of one wall. When shadows moved across the wall, they made it seem as if the leaves on the tree were rustling, as if the whole wallpaper garden was moving, slithering.

"The wallpaper is grotesque," Zenobia agreed. "And not even pleasantly grotesque. But"—she firmly closed both eyes—"you'll never learn to sense the Spirits, Elizabeth, if you remain so concerned with earthly details like wallpaper."

I tried not to look at the wallpaper.

But then something in it made me start.

A pair of eyes.

They belonged to a girl. A wallpaper girl. A girl, maybe a little younger than me, who was looking out at me from the wallpaper just to the left of the windowsill.

But not really looking at me, I told myself. How could she be looking at me? She was part of the paper's pattern, nothing more.

All the same, I decided I had spent enough time in the nursery.

"Zenobia . . . ," I began.

Zenobia's head was tipped back, and her hands trembled. She murmured incantations under her breath.

"Zenobia, I really think we should—"

"Not now, Elizabeth." Zenobia spoke from the side of her mouth. "The Presence is about to reveal itself."

A shadow fell across the room. My insides went cold.

"It's here!" cried Zenobia. "The Spirit Presence!" She rushed toward the shadow with open arms. Then she stopped. Her arms fell back to her sides.

The shadow belonged to Mrs. Purswell, who was standing before the window. She had come into the room without either of us noticing. Zenobia was right. Mrs. Purswell really *had* made an art of lurking.

"I rang the bell for tea nearly fifteen minutes ago," she said. She moved to the door and motioned for me to follow. "I will tell your father you were in the library, reading something of a scientific nature. I will tell him you were so engrossed in your reading, you didn't hear me ring."

"Yes, Mrs. Purswell," I said, hoping that she didn't notice Zenobia stamping her foot and crying, "How am I supposed to connect with the Spirit Presence when I am constantly being interrupted?" Zenobia glared at the door. It squealed on its hinges and slammed shut.

Only not quite. Mrs. Purswell stopped it with one leather shoe squarely in the doorframe.

"It's only natural," she continued as if nothing had happened, "that you should be curious to explore your new house. But the East Wing is forbidden to you, as you know. I'm sure I won't find you here again."

"No, Mrs. Purswell."

I followed Mrs. Purswell through the corridor, past the por-traits, down the stairs that led back to the tapestry, and out of the East Wing.

Zenobia lagged behind me.

"Elizabeth!" she called. "Elizabeth!"

"What is it?" I kept my voice very quiet. Zenobia held out the flower. It wasn't wilted. In fact, it was quite the opposite. I stopped and put a hand out to its petals. They had burst into blossom. Its leaves had grown big and turned a green so vivid they practically glowed. It had become the biggest and most beautiful rose I had ever seen.

What could it mean, the flower bursting into life like that? I thought to myself.

"I don't know." Zenobia frowned at the flower. "But I know it means something."

5
The Garden

After breakfast, Mrs. Purswell appeared and took my marmalade knife and my crumb-strewn plate. But instead of carrying them back to the kitchen, she stood before me and said in a firm voice, "It's a lovely day, Miss Elizabeth."

"Oh, yes," I said. "It's sunny for once. It's the first sunny day since I came to Witheringe House, in fact."

"I would go outside, if I had the chance to, on a day like today. I would go outside and enjoy the sunshine."

"Well," I said, "perhaps I—"

"I certainly wouldn't rattle around in the house. And I would steer very clear indeed of the East Wing. Oh, yes, I'd go out. Into the garden."

She stood there, waiting, I realized, for me to say something.

"Thank you," I said. "What an excellent—um—suggestion."

———◆———

Outside, I tipped my face to the sky and let the sun warm it.

"You know," said Zenobia, "when you smile like that, you look rather simple."

"It's difficult not to smile," I said, "on such a nice day."

"I don't see anything nice about it." She was wearing dark-tinted glasses and she stood huddled under a black silk parasol. The glasses and parasol were measures, she explained, to ward off the sunshine. "I find sunshine," she said, "rather vulgar. At least"—she let her glasses slide down the bridge of her nose so she could look at me over the top of them—"the garden is atmospheric enough."

Atmospheric! The word I would have chosen was "dead." The trees were bare and the lawn was bald. The only things that thrived in this garden were weeds. Weeds that choked the bowl of the birdbath and seemed to crawl underfoot.

We walked, in the shadow of the house, up a sloped path that took us through rows of worm-eaten rose bushes.

"What do you suppose," asked Zenobia, "is a respectable amount of time to walk about in the garden?"

"A respectable amount of time?"

"Before we sneak back inside."

"Sneak back inside?"

Even though she wore tinted glasses, I could tell Zenobia was rolling her eyes.

"I really do have to spell everything out for you, don't I?" She spoke loudly and clearly, as if to a very small child. "To sneak back inside and continue our search for the Spirit Presence in the East Wing."

"I don't know if that's such a good idea," I said. "Look." I pointed up to the house, at the dark shape silhouetted at one of the windows of the dining room.

Mrs. Purswell stood looking out into the garden, at the place where we stood looking back at her.

"We're stuck out here, then," sighed Zenobia. "How tedious. You know, I really sensed something in the nursery. It seemed filled with the Spirit Presence. It was positively—well—positively haunted."

I nudged a dried tuft of grass with the tip of my shoe.

The truth was, I had felt the hauntedness, too. I had felt it as we stood in the nursery's thick, dark air. And the feeling had stayed with me, even after we'd closed the door behind us. It was a strange feeling, unpleasant and lingering and sticky, like the feeling of having walked into a cobweb.

"No," I lied. I didn't want to encourage Zenobia. "It didn't seem haunted to me."

She sniffed. "I'm just more sensitive to these kinds of things than you."

We wandered through the garden. I stopped to pick a flower that proved, on closer inspection, a weed. Then I crouched and watched a snail inch across the earth in front of me. Zenobia stopped only once, to pluck up a bird skull from the ground. "It's just the thing to counteract the blueness of our bedroom," she explained.

We came upon the sundial. Zenobia inspected the shadow that fell across its stone face. "Half-past nine," she said. "Quarter to ten at the very latest." And she flipped open her watch to check. "Nine thirty-three to be precise. Which means hours till Mrs. Purswell lets us inside for lunch."

"Are you bored of the garden already? If you like, we could play—"

"Play? You know I don't play, Elizabeth."

"A picnic, then? We could make moss sandwiches. It might be fun."

"A *picnic*?" Zenobia pressed a melodramatic hand to her forehead. "I think I'm going to be ill."

"Real people like picnics," I muttered.

Luckily, Zenobia didn't hear me. She was distracted by a clump of hedge, the one I had seen from the window on our first morning at Witheringe House.

"It's a maze!" she called. "A hedge maze!"

I walked to the hedge. I could see it had once been cut into a maze. But now the hedges were bare and so badly overgrown that only a thin path needled between them. The bare branches of the tree at its center reached out over the ragged hedgerow and made a shape like a fork of lightning.

"Aren't hedge mazes supposed to be sort of . . . green?" I asked. "And not so sharp-looking?"

"Green is a color much overrated in gardens," Zenobia announced. "I prefer this gray brown." She slipped through the opening and into the maze. "Are you coming in?"

I paused.

"You said you wanted to do something fun," she said. "Well, here's your chance."

"I guess it might be fun." I looked at the maze doubtfully. "Puzzles are fun, after all. And a maze is just a kind of puzzle, really."

"Exactly," said Zenobia. She snapped her parasol shut and disappeared into the hedges.

I pushed through after her. Thorns tugged at my clothes. The branches were so thick and twisted, I couldn't see the sun through them.

"Keep your eyes peeled," Zenobia said over her shoulder. "We might see the skeletons . . . of those who went before us and"—she made her voice low and spooky—"never came out."

I knew she was joking, but I wished she wouldn't say such things. Already, I had lost sight of the way we had come in. If only I had stayed outside, safe, in the garden.

"Who said I was joking?" she called back to me.

I almost hated Zenobia, right at that moment. I wanted nothing more than to be far, far away from her and the cruel ways she made fun of my fears. But I wanted, just as much, to be as close to her as possible, to be reassured I wasn't alone in this dark—and getting darker—maze.

So I stayed close, close enough that I could feel the hem of her skirt swishing against the front of my legs.

"Ooh!" She went up on tiptoe. "I just caught a glimpse of the center."

"Where?" I strained to see.

"We'll be there soon. You know, there are old stories of mazes used to trap terrible monsters."

"Don't," I said softly.

"Like the Minotaur," she went on, "in the labyrinth. If anyone was unlucky enough to get lost in the labyrinth, then the Minotaur would eat them."

I swallowed hard. "Stop, Zenobia. That's enough."

"Crunch on their bones," she said. "Suck on their blood."

The hedges on either side of me pressed too close. "Please stop!" My voice was hoarse. "I don't want to hear any more."

Zenobia turned and looked at me scornfully. "I said it was just a story, didn't I?"

"Stories can be scary, too," I whispered.

The hedge opened out into a clearing at the center of the maze. A dark, twisty shape rose up. I gasped and hid myself as best I could against the scratchy hedge, until Zenobia found me and dragged me into the clearing.

"See?" She pointed. "There's no monster. Only a tree. A very fine-looking tree, if you ask me."

Up close, the tree only looked even more horrible than it had from afar. It was gray and bare, and its roots had come all unstuck from the ground. They waved, brittle and bone-pale, in the air.

"I always *do* prefer dead trees," said Zenobia, "to living ones. There's something so starkly dramatic about dead trees, I always think."

"Not quite dead," I said, and I showed her a thin strand of roots that still stretched from the base of the trunk into the soil.

Zenobia prodded the roots with the point of her shoe. "But not alive for much longer, I shouldn't think."

I looked at my scuffed shoes and my torn stockings. The twisted tree roots gave me a twisted feeling in my stomach.

Zenobia made a face. "Honestly, Elizabeth, only *you* would be scared of a *tree*."

Still, she went faster going out of the maze than she had going in, and she gave my hand a quick squeeze when I stumbled out after her into the garden.

———◆———

We walked together, up the path that led right to the end of the garden. It grew steeper and steeper until it reached the top of the hill. There the garden stopped and the earth dropped away sharply. Beyond were fields of long grass punctuated by stone fences. In the distance we could see a spindled spire and a handful of slate roofs that belonged, I guessed, to the houses of Witheringe Green.

In one of the fields was a figure, head bent down. It was Father. He stooped to inspect something. A flower? A fern? I was too far away to tell. He took out his notebook and wrote in it. My heart lifted a little inside me.

I watched him for a while, until rain splattered in my hair and over my shoulders. I tipped my face to the sky, which was now hung with heavy clouds.

Zenobia grinned triumphantly at the darkening sky. "Mrs. Purswell can hardly expect you to stay outside now! Quickly"— she tugged on my sleeve—"to the East Wing, and the Spirit Presence! If we hurry, we can lift the Veil to the World Beyond before tea!"

She started back to the house, pulling me after her. But the rain grew heavier and wind started to whip.

Soon the rain was like a sheet of glass in front of us. I couldn't see the house through it.

But there, on the ridge, was the falling-down shed I had seen from the blue guest bedroom window. I tugged at Zenobia's wrist and I dragged her toward it. "In here," I said.

The shed, when we reached it, was dirty and green with moss on the outside. But inside it was warm. Its walls and floor were covered in plants. They climbed over trellises and filled flower-pots. Real, green, living plants. I took a breath in, and the smell and taste of soil filled my lungs.

"What is this place?" I wondered aloud.

"It's the nursery" came a voice. A deep, soft voice that slith-ered snakelike over the "s" sounds.

I started. Even Zenobia started. She let her bird skull fall from her hand, then quickly retrieved it.

Looking through the plants, I saw that the voice belonged to a man. His skin was white and shiny, like the skin of an onion or a leek. I couldn't decide if he was very old or very young. He wore a soil-clotted shirt and faded old gardening gloves. He was stand-ing at a workbench in the middle of the room. Before him was a potted plant. It was very beautiful. Its leaves were pale green, and peeking out from between them were pale pink flowers with petals as ruffly as lace petticoats.

"I'm sorry," I said. "I didn't mean to interrupt you."

"That's quite all right," said the man, and I noticed how pleasant his voice was in my ears. "This is your house, after all, Miss Elizabeth. I am only the gardener. May I say, it's good to have your father back at Witheringe House, and you here with him. But you are without your mother?"

"She left," I said.

"People sometimes do," he said mildly. "They're not rooted in the soil, the way plants are."

He smiled in a way that made me want to stand closer to him. I went over to the workbench. Zenobia did, too. The plants rustled as we moved through them.

Up close, the plant with the lacy pink flowers smelled like powdered sugar. Zenobia wrinkled her nose. "The stench in here," she announced, "is intolerable." She slipped into one of the nursery's mossy, dank corners.

I stayed where I was, admiring the plant.

"You like it, then?" asked the gardener.

"Yes," I said. "I like it very much. I don't think I've ever seen one quite like it before."

The gardener smiled. "It's a very fine specimen," he said. Then he wrapped one gloved hand around the plant and ripped it from its soil. He held it up so I could see its thin, tangled roots.

"What are you doing?" I cried.

"Grafting," he said. He reached for a large rusted set of shears and cut the plant from its roots. The squeak and scrape of the shears through the plant's stem made a sound like a shriek— almost like the poor plant was crying out in pain.

"Grafting seems awfully cruel," I said.

"You wouldn't say that, Miss Elizabeth, if you knew how it worked. Grafting is when you take two plants and join them together. This one here is the rootstock." He lifted a large shrub with a bulbous trunk and knobbled branches onto the table. "It's got a good, strong set of roots. See?" And with his index finger, he eased one of the roots out of the soil. It was as thick as my thumb. Then he patted it back down.

"And this"—he pointed at the other plant, with its parts laid out on the table—"is the cultivar. A shoot of the cultivar is joined onto the rootstock, like so." He took a length of twine and bound the green stem tightly to the stem of the rootstock, cutting into the shoot so sharply with the twine that it broke open, bleeding sap. "And after a while they'll twist and twine together. The two plants will grow so close together, in fact, that after a time, they'll just be the one plant. A plant that blossoms with beautiful pink flowers. A plant with thick, strong roots that will live a long time in the soil where it's planted."

I gathered the broken parts of the green flowering plant toward me. "It still doesn't seem very nice for the clut—the curl—"

"The cultivar," he corrected, and he smiled again—such a kind smile—and swept the plant cuttings onto the floor.

He reached once more for the shears, and I looked away. I didn't want to watch any more of the grafting. "I think," I said, "I've interrupted you long enough."

I looked around for Zenobia, but she had disappeared among the plants.

There was a clattering from a far corner of the shed. "Just some pots," Zenobia said as she emerged from the greenery. "I may have kicked them over accidentally. But look!" She held up a dead beetle, with one of its sharp pincers dangling askew, and a handful of dead leaves. "They'll go with the bird skull nicely."

I looked over my shoulder as I went outside. "It was nice to meet you," I said to the gardener.

"Likewise," he said, still smiling.

The rain was just a drizzle now. We walked back to the house through fine, wet mist.

"Do you think the nursery was a little strange?" I asked Zenobia.

"In what way strange?"

"It's so wonderful and green and good-smelling in there. It doesn't feel like it belongs to Witheringe House at all."

"There are plenty of green things here in the garden," Zenobia said.

"Weeds and nettles," I said. "No plants, no flowers."

"The plants in the nursery were altogether too bright and fragrant if you ask me," sniffed Zenobia. "The only plant I liked was that Frankenstein-plant. It was quite grotesque, I thought, the way the gardener grafted the two of them together. Quite wonderfully *brutal*."

I said nothing. I hadn't liked the grafting at all—I felt sure it must have been painful for the poor pink-flowered plant. I knew it was silly of me. After all, the gardener had been so kind. And he *had* explained that grafting was good for the plant. But I couldn't stop hearing the shriek of the plant snapping between the shears.

Father didn't come down for lunch. But he was there at dinner. He sat in his usual place, at the opposite end of the table from me.

"How was your day, Father?" I made my voice as loud as it would go.

"Productive," he said. He put down his fork. "I spent the afternoon with some extremely interesting specimens of various *Asteraceae*. I think there may be some important connections between the *Agrianthus* and the *Leucoptera* that have been overlooked in previous studies." He returned to his corned beef and spent quite a long time working his knife through the leathery meat.

I assumed our conversation was finished. But then he looked up at me and said, "And what about you, Elizabeth? I'm afraid I've left you too much to your own devices since we arrived. Are you settling in well to Witheringe House?"

"It's different from the old house," I said. "But I think I could grow to like it. And the garden is much bigger."

He swallowed hard and dabbed his moustache with his napkin. "The garden's in a state of disrepair, I'm afraid."

"I'm sure the gardener will see to it," I said.

"What gardener, Elizabeth?"

"The gardener. I was in the garden today. I met him. In the nursery."

Father crumpled his napkin and put it by his plate. "Mrs. Purswell," he said.

Mrs. Purswell stood suddenly beside him.

"Like magic," said Zenobia admiringly. "You merely need to say her name and"—she snapped her fingers—"there she is!"

"Mrs. Purswell," said Father, "have you engaged a gardener?"

"I'm yet to find anyone suitable, Dr. Murmur," she said.

"Then why does Elizabeth tell me she met with the gardener today?"

"I can't say, sir. There's certainly no gardener here."

Father frowned at me down the length of the table. "You know it's wrong to lie, Elizabeth."

"I'm not lying! I saw him! And Zenobia did, too!"

"Enough." Father pushed his plate away. "This has gone on long enough."

Father spent the rest of the evening alone in the library.

———————◆———————

That night, I couldn't sleep. At last, I groped in the dark for the candle and for *The Plant Kingdom*. I sat up against my pillow and opened the book.

I read along with the chiming of the clock.

At eleven thirty I was reading about herbaceous perennials. By eleven forty-five I had progressed to annuals. And then, as the clock struck midnight, I turned the page and was met with the same green, looping script that I had seen—or dreamed—when I had last read the book.

The Kingdom rejoiced with the birth of the new Prince. At the palace, the flag, which was really a red geranium and not a flag at all, was run up the pole. Every flower in the kingdom burst into bloom, and the bees turned giddy with all the pollen.

The boy grew up to be lovely and loved by all. But on the day of his seventh birthday, he became ill. He turned from green to pale green to nearly white, and his face closed up with pain. The King sent away the grasshoppers he had engaged to play at the celebration and cancelled the rain of rose petals that was to follow the cutting of the cake. The head gardener was called, but he could find nothing wrong—until he turned the

Prince's roots out of the soil and found them spotted and turning soft and shriveled at their ends. That night, the young Prince died.

On the next page the looping green writing stopped. I fluttered my fingers through the rest of the book, but all I saw was the dense black type of before. I turned back to find the page written in green. It wasn't there anymore. I wondered if I had really seen it at all.

I blew out the candle and laid my head on the pillow, feeling sure I wouldn't sleep. But I must have slept, because soon I fell into a dream.

In the dream I was wandering through the hedge maze, alone. The branches caught at my sleeves and my hair. It felt like the maze wanted to swallow me up.

I woke in a tangle of sheets.

I had just climbed out of bed when Mrs. Purswell appeared at my door. "Your father wishes to see you," she said. She looked at the hairbrush in my hand and my stockinged feet. "Immediately."

I jammed my feet into my shoes without lacing them and left my hair unbrushed and ran to Father's study.

I stood at the door, gathering my nerves.

It was open a crack, and I could see Father at his desk. He was surrounded by flowers. Flowers with cottony white petals and blue star–shaped flowers in specimen jars. Dried flowers tacked onto pieces of card were scattered over his desk. His head was bent over a book. I was glad to see him at work again—and sorry I would have to interrupt.

"Please sit," said Father when I entered, and I did. He put down his pen and turned to look at me. "Elizabeth," he said. "Perhaps I haven't been as attentive as I should have been since—well—since everything happened."

Since Mother left, he meant.

"You're lonely," he continued. "And it's not unusual for a lonely child to imagine herself somehow less lonely. Zenobia. The gardener. I understand why you imagine them, why it might be comforting for you to think they exist."

"I've explained to you," I said in a hard voice, "that Zenobia is not imaginary."

"But I've indulged these imaginings long enough," he said, as if I'd not spoken at all. "I have engaged a governess. She'll take your lessons in hand—they've been neglected since we arrived at Witheringe House. And she'll be a companion for you."

"I don't want a companion."

"She'll help you forget about Zenobia."

"I'm not going to forget about Zenobia."

He held up his hand to show I should stop talking.

"It's for the best," he said.

He turned back to his book. This meant the conversation was

over. There was nothing left for me to do but walk slowly back down the hall.

Two days later Miss Clemency arrived, with a small traveling case, a large hatbox, and a glowing letter of recommendation from the Mrs. Aurelia Smythe School for Superior Governesses held out in one of her primly gloved hands.

She was shown around the crumbling house and the dead garden, and after the tour, she pronounced them both "charming." She complimented Mrs. Purswell on her cooking and drew a rare smile from Father at the dinner table with an anecdote about her time at the Mrs. Aurelia Smythe School for Superior Governesses that involved a spilled inkwell, an escaped milking goat, and a Pillar of Society. And when the plates were cleared, she insisted on taking the dust sheet off the piano, declaring, "Music is beneficial to the digestion." She filled the cold, empty ballroom with a song that, at my request, used only the white keys. Father turned the pages for her. Even Mrs. Purswell, in a corner of the room, moved her head in time to the music.

Zenobia hated her immediately.

6
Miss Clemency

My lessons with Miss Clemency began the next day. The music room was converted to a schoolroom. Miss Clemency's desk was in front of the blackboard. Mine was by the window. Zenobia perched on the windowsill.

"I think," said Miss Clemency, a stick of chalk poised in her fingers, "we'll begin with geometry. After all, the sooner we start it, the sooner we'll finish it!"

"Why does she insist on baring her teeth at us?" Zenobia asked.

"She's smiling," I whispered.

"Are you sure she's smiling? Are you sure she's not snarling?"

Miss Clemency drew a series of triangles on the board. "Now," she said brightly. "What do you know about the Greek mathematician Pythagoras?"

"He was stoned to death by an angry mob," said Zenobia.

"Nothing," I said, loudly and hurriedly. "Nothing at all."

"Well," said Miss Clemency, "he invented a very charming rule for measuring my favorite shape, the triangle."

I whispered the rule under my breath as I worked the problems Miss Clemency set for me. "The square of the hypotenuse," I chanted to myself, "is equal to the squares of the other two sides combined. The square of the hypotenuse is equal to the squares of the other two sides combined."

Zenobia smiled in a satisfied way when Miss Clemency took up my book to check it. I knew at once she had worked some mischief in it. Miss Clemency returned the book to my desk without saying a word. There, on the page opposite my triangles, was a drawing of Miss Clemency. Zenobia had made her eyes round like saucers and turned her pupils cross-eyed. Her mouth was wide and full of teeth, like a shark's.

"It was Zenobia!" The words jumped out before I could stop them. I clamped a hand over my lips.

"Your father told me about Zenobia," said Miss Clemency, "and I can see she is quite a talented artist. Perhaps you and I and Zenobia will have a drawing lesson after tea."

I secretly narrowed my eyes at Zenobia. "That sounds wonderful," I said, making my smile sparkle the same way Miss Clemency's did.

"We have to get rid of her." Zenobia sat on the blue bedspread in the blue bedroom. "The question is, how?"

I was unfurling the sketches I had made that afternoon, spreading them on the blue carpet—a hedgehog, a clump of ferns, a grasshopper. I had drawn the grasshopper lopsided, I saw now, but I was still proud of the way I had done its antennae.

"I don't want to get rid of her," I answered, though my voice rose at the end of the sentence so it seemed more like a question.

Zenobia slowly lifted her left eyebrow. I felt the room turn cold and I pulled the fabric of my nightdress close around me.

"I like her," I said, and this time I kept my voice firm.

The cold in the room grew sharper and a wind picked up out of nowhere. It whipped my hair across my face and into my mouth and tore the windows open. The drawings on the carpet lifted up and hovered in the air.

"Zenobia!" I sprang to my feet and tried to snatch them, but each time I came close to one of the papers it flew out of my reach. The wind grew stronger still and I watched as, one by one, the drawings floated higher and then higher again and then out of the open windows and into the night.

The wind calmed.

The room lost its chill.

The windows closed.

"That was uncalled for," I said in a tight voice.

"They weren't very good, anyway," said Zenobia. "That grasshopper was lopsided, in case you hadn't noticed."

She drew back the blue bedspread and opened *The World Beyond*. She pretended to be absorbed in Chapter Seven: "Spirit Rapping, Psychography, and Basic Necromancy." She pretended not to hear me when I said good night.

Zenobia's campaign to scare away Miss Clemency started out small. Things happened in lessons that Miss Clemency could easily blame on the wind or on her own absentmindedness. Like the books whose pages ruffled back and forth whenever she found the passage she wanted to read from. Or the paintings on the walls that came free from their hooks and suddenly fell to the floor. Or the time she took off her hat and later couldn't find it anywhere, not in the drawers of her desk or the hook by the door, until Mrs. Purswell came in wanting to know why Miss Clemency had left her hat beside the hams in the pantry.

And, for the first time in forever, Zenobia and I weren't talking. Or rather, we were talking, but our conversations were guarded and never turned to the topic of Miss Clemency.

I couldn't prove, then, that any of the incidents were Zenobia's doing, but I had my suspicions. And these were confirmed during one drawing lesson when Miss Clemency opened her paint box to find all the tubes of paint gone, and in their place, very smelly and very stiff, a dead mouse.

As Miss Clemency opened the box, Zenobia leaned in close, with a smile starting on her lips, to see what she would do. But Miss Clemency merely removed the mouse and said, "On second thought, we will work with charcoals today."

I turned my back to Zenobia while I sketched. My fingers turned gray and then black with the charcoal.

"That wasn't funny," I told her after the lesson.

"Well, it wasn't *meant* to be funny." She flounced off.

"I know what you're trying to do," I called after her. "And I don't like it at all."

When Miss Clemency fell into step beside me, I realized she must have heard me calling out—calling into thin air as far as she knew. I put my hands over my cheeks so she wouldn't see the redness spreading over them and said, "I was just telling Zenobia not to—well, the dead mouse. That was her. I didn't have anything to do with that."

"I never thought for a moment you did."

I looked up at her. "You won't leave, will you?"

"Leave?"

"Because of the—"

"Because of the mouse?" Her laugh pealed like a bell. "I covered rodents, dead and alive, as well as arachnids, insects, and amphibians, on my very first morning of classes at the School for Superior Governesses. It takes much more than a dead mouse to scare *me*."

And, true to her word, she didn't bat an eyelid when the top drawer of her desk filled with soil and squirming earthworms. Or when the African continent disappeared altogether from the pages of her atlas. Or when she went to walk to the blackboard but found her shoes would only take her to the window.

I started to think Miss Clemency, with her placid manner and her twinkling smile, might prove to be Zenobia's match.

Zenobia's pranks grew more and more desperate—but it seemed there was nothing she could do to ruffle Miss Clemency's calm.

Until one rainy Thursday morning.

It was time for my history lesson. Miss Clemency stood at the blackboard. Zenobia stared straight at Miss Clemency. Her eyes, I saw, were brightly focused. I should have known she was plotting something far beyond her usual mischief.

"Today is a special day"—Miss Clemency drew a stick of chalk from its box—"because today we are going to learn about one of the most remarkable persons ever to have lived."

She wrote on the board, "Leonardo da Vinci." As she dotted the last "i," the blackboard shivered and shook against the wall. Miss Clemency steadied it.

"Now," she asked, "what do you already know about Signor da Vinci?"

I remembered a painting from a book of a half-smiling lady with her hands folded in her lap.

"He was an artist," I said.

"Well done, Elizabeth!" Miss Clemency glowed. I could feel myself glowing in return. "He *was* an artist," she said. "His most famous painting is, of course, the *Mona Lisa*. But he was much more besides."

The blackboard rattled against the wall. Miss Clemency clicked her tongue. "This wind," she said, and she pulled the window shut.

"Leonardo da Vinci," she continued, "was also an engineer. A scientist. An inventor. An inventor of large things."

On the blackboard she drew a strange contraption. It looked like a mechanical bird.

"Da Vinci's famous flying machine," she explained. "Centuries before those clever Wright Brothers, Leonardo da Vinci dreamed up an airplane of his own."

The blackboard banged heavily against the wall. A fine rain of chalk dust turned Miss Clemency's hair a ghostly white.

"Da Vinci," she continued, "was an inventor of small things, too. Like this."

The blackboard rattled and banged so violently, Miss Clemency could hardly write on it. She steadied it with one hand and wrote with the other.

I turned to Zenobia. Her hands were balled into fists. Her lips moved around silent words. Her eyes never left the blackboard.

There was a sharp, creaking sound.

A crack appeared at the top of the blackboard.

"Miss Clemency!" I cried. My desk clattered to the floor as I leaped forward. I grabbed Miss Clemency by the elbow and pulled her backward, just as the blackboard cracked in two. The right half was left hanging askew on the wall. The left half fell with a bang to the floor—over the very place where Miss Clemency had been standing.

Miss Clemency gasped. Zenobia was slumped, pale and exhausted, in her chair, but her face was split with a triumphant grin.

And then Miss Clemency collected herself. She pushed the left half of the blackboard up against the wall.

"Now," she said, "where were we? Ah, yes—another of da Vinci's inventions. It's a secret code of sorts. Do you think you can decode it, Elizabeth?"

I glanced back at Zenobia on my way to the board. Her grin had fallen away. Her pleased expression had curdled. She looked defeated. I almost could have felt sorry for Zenobia just then. Almost, but not quite. I turned my back firmly to her when I reached the board.

I studied the script Miss Clemency had drawn on the blackboard. Its letters looked nearly like letters I knew, but I couldn't decipher them.

"I don't think so," I told her.

"Have you ever noticed a very charming thing about mirrors—namely, that a mirror will always show the reverse of what stands before it? So what appears rightwise in real life will be leftwise in a mirror. And what, in real life, is leftwise—"

"A mirror will show rightwise," I finished.

"Very good," she said. She pulled a mirrored compact from her pocket, flicked it open, and handed it to me. "See if you can decode it now."

I held the compact up to the script. In the mirror, the letters spelled two words: *Mirror Writing.*

"Da Vinci used mirror writing in all of his notebooks," said Miss Clemency. "Wasn't that cunning?"

Zenobia let her chair fall to the floor with a bang. She stomped across the room. As loud as thunder, she slammed the door behind her.

"That was Zenobia, just now," I said. "The door. The blackboard. She doesn't mean to be so awful—or she does, but she wouldn't if she only knew how nice you were."

"Well," said Miss Clemency. "It's nice of *you* to think I'm nice, Elizabeth. Whatever Zenobia's opinion of me may be."

Zenobia didn't appear for tea that day. Mrs. Purswell still set a plate for her beside me.

Looking at Zenobia's empty plate and her empty chair, I wasn't sure if I felt angry or sad.

I remembered the loud way the blackboard had cracked in half and how it had fallen inches from Miss Clemency's head.

I decided I felt angry.

"That was a cruel trick," I told her that night in the blue bed-room. "And dangerous, too."

Zenobia looked up from *The World Beyond* by Famed and Celebrated Clairvoyant Madame Lucent.

"You could have badly hurt Miss Clemency," I said.

"I wouldn't have *badly* hurt her, Elizabeth," she said. "Just scared her enough to make her leave Witheringe House and never come back."

"Why do you dislike her so much?" I asked.

"Why do *you* like her so much?" she spat.

"It's because I like her, isn't it?" I buttoned my nightgown. "You dislike her *because* I like her."

"I hardly think so," said Zenobia in an icy tone.

The room turned suddenly cold. I shivered, and my fingers trembled as I did up my last button.

"Well, I'm not going to stop liking her on your account," I said through chattering teeth.

The chill in the room sharpened. Silently, I took another blanket down from the wardrobe and wrapped it around me. In bed, I turned away from Zenobia.

I went to sleep trembling from the cold. Next morning when I woke, I was trembling still.

"Zenobia has decided not to come to class again," I told Miss Clemency the next day. "She said conventional lessons were tedious for someone of her elevated interests and abilities and that they distract her from her true purpose at Witheringe House."

"I see," said Miss Clemency. "And do you mind me asking, what *is* Zenobia's true purpose at Witheringe House?"

I moved close to Miss Clemency and made my voice into a whisper. "She thinks there's a ghost here," I explained. "Only she says we shouldn't use the word 'ghost,' that the correct nomenclature is 'Spirit Presence.' She has sensed a Spirit Presence, and she wants to commune—that is, talk—with it."

"Do you believe there is a ghost—or a Spirit Presence, I should say?" asked Miss Clemency.

"Father says there's no such things as ghosts."

"And do you agree?"

I thought for a moment. "I'm scared of them," I said, "if that's the same as believing in them. Father says you can't believe in something you can't see. But no one else can see Zenobia, and I know she's real. Do you believe in Zenobia, Miss Clemency?"

It was her turn to think. "I believe you are an honest girl, Elizabeth," she said after a while. "And I believe you wouldn't tell me, or your father, or anyone else for that matter, an untruth. So it follows that . . . that yes, I do believe in Zenobia."

If I hadn't felt so shy about it, I would have hugged Miss Clemency. Instead, I took one of her gloved hands in both of my own, and I squeezed it tightly.

Zenobia didn't appear for tea that day either. I was still angry when I looked at her empty plate. But there was something else, something uncomfortable, behind the anger: the feeling that some small but vital part of me was missing and that I could never feel whole without it.

I pushed the feeling away. I concentrated on my turnip stew, instead.

The days after that one fell into a kind of routine. Father worked, spending each morning in the fields and each afternoon in his study, and the house was soon filled with flowers: in the library, in the drawing room, even some, in specimen jars, on Miss Clemency's desk, where she took pleasure in rearranging them and brushing her fingers across their petals during breaks in my lessons.

After tea each day, Miss Clemency took me for drawing lessons, and once, leaning over a self-portrait still missing its left ear, she said I was becoming "quite a skilled artist."

Zenobia kept on in her quest to commune with the Spirit Presence, pointedly leaving me out of all her efforts in this direction. I was glad for the reprieve, though the haunted feeling I'd had in the nursery still lingered darkly at the edges of my mind.

"Still enjoying your lessons?" she asked one evening in the blue guest bedroom.

"Still poking about in the East Wing, trying to find your ghost?" I shot back.

"Actually," she said with some dignity, "my search for the Spirit Presence has led me further afield."

I wouldn't understand just how much further afield Zenobia had gone until the next afternoon.

Miss Clemency had declared the light was "very good indeed" and that we should have our drawing lesson outside. We went out of the house and up the hill. We stood on its ridge, looking back down toward the house, and we drew what we could see before us.

The first thing I drew was a squirrel, flashing red in the branches of a tree. It took three tries before I was satisfied with my picture. Then I drew a cloud that had nearly the same shape as a shoe, and I had just picked up my green crayon to start on a tangled box hedge when I sensed a movement behind me.

Zenobia stood at my elbow. "When will you finish?" she said.

I looked at my paper. "I haven't begun yet," I said.

"You need to come with me. There's something you have to see."

"Perhaps I don't want to come with you." I outlined the hedge. "After all, you haven't been especially nice to me recently."

"It's important," she insisted.

I shaded a patch of green leaves. I made no sign I had heard her. How typical of Zenobia, I thought. She had treated me so coldly these last few days. Now, as soon as she wanted something from me, she expected that we should be friends again, without her even apologizing.

"I'm *sorry*, then," she hissed.

"Sorry for what?" I hissed back.

"I'm sorry I've been disagreeable to you."

"Not just to me," I reminded her.

"I'm sorry I was disagreeable to Miss Clemency, too, then. There. Are you happy?"

I was. I was happy Zenobia had apologized. And happier still to have my friend back.

I crumpled up my paper. "Miss Clemency—"

Miss Clemency turned, her paintbrush, dripping pastel pink, halfway to her paper. "Yes, Elizabeth?"

"Zenobia has something important to show me."

"Very well." Miss Clemency wiped her brush clean on the grass and fastened her hat to her head. "If it's important, I'd best come with you."

Zenobia went over the top of the hill, putting the house quickly behind her.

"This way." I pointed for Miss Clemency, and together we followed her.

JESSICA MILLER

"Where are we going?" I asked when we were halfway down the other side of the hill. Zenobia didn't answer. She just kept walking, as dark and purposeful as a swarm of bees. I sped up, and Miss Clemency sped up beside me.

On the downward slope of the hill, the ground came away so fast beneath my feet, I felt I was flying. Finally, we came to a narrow road, crossing the flattish place where our hill joined another.

"This way," said Zenobia, and she started down the road.

I waited for Miss Clemency, who was walking with her skirts bunched up about her knees, and beckoned her to follow. In the distance a collection of shapes came together to form the slate tiled roofs and the spindling church spire of Witheringe Green.

It didn't take long to walk from one end of the main street to the other. We passed some houses with neat gardens and shuttered windows, a haberdasher with faded bolts of fabric in the window, an apothecary with its sign shaped like a mortar and pestle, a seed shop selling packets of sweet peas, runner beans, and geraniums.

Zenobia stopped at last in front of a small stone church. "In here," she said. We walked through an overgrown garden and around to the back of the building where, cut into the foot of a hill, was a modest graveyard, with rows of small crooked

98

crosses and plain tombstones with most of the inscriptions on them worn away. Zenobia rested her hand on the iron gate that led into the graveyard for a moment, then pushed. It opened with a creak and her white fingers came away dusted orange with rust. She went through and motioned for me to follow.

I stopped, with one foot over the step. I registered the familiar signs of fear—the dry mouth, the light stomach, the heartbeat that I could feel everywhere in my body: behind my eyes, at the backs of my knees.

"Oh, come on, Elizabeth," snapped Zenobia. She grabbed a handful of my dress and tried to pull me in, but I didn't move. "There's absolutely nothing to be afraid of—I've always found graveyards to be—"

But before she could finish, Miss Clemency spoke. "Come on, Elizabeth," she soothed. "There's absolutely nothing to be afraid of." She looked at a crumbling stone angel whose left hand had fallen off, and at the low-hanging branches of the oak tree that shaded the rows of graves. "I've always found graveyards to be quite beautiful"—and here, Zenobia looked up at her in surprise—"in a melancholy kind of way." And Miss Clemency unwrapped my fingers from where they were hooked around the gate and led me inside. "Now," she said, "I wonder what Zenobia has to show us."

Zenobia walked up to the marble tombstone of a grave set apart from the others, and there she stopped. I could see the place where a hand had pushed away the ferns and weeds growing over it to make the inscription visible.

Tourmaline, aged seven years.
Beloved daughter of Edward and Lydia.
Adored sister of Henry.

7
Tourmaline

I was sitting at the dinner table, looking at a plate of stringy cabbage stew, but in my head I was still at the cemetery. I was still kneeling before the headstone, staring at the words etched across it.

"'Tourmaline,'" I had said softly to myself. "'Adored sister of Henry.' Tourmaline Murmur. Sister of Henry Murmur. But Henry Murmur is my—"

I had felt a light hand on my shoulder. "Did you know your father had a sister?" asked Miss Clemency.

I had shaken my head. I didn't know.

And yet I wanted to know—there was so much I desperately wanted to know.

How had Tourmaline died?

And why had she been kept a secret?

I remembered the dedication at the front of Father's book. I remembered the nursery with its two narrow beds. One for Father and the other, of course, for Tourmaline. I remembered, too, the uneasy feeling that had stuck to my skin ever since I first went in there.

Was it Tourmaline who was giving the nursery its haunted feeling?

Was Father haunted by her, too?

I looked down the table to Father. His cabbage stew sat uneaten. He was too busy talking to raise the loaded fork in his hand to his mouth.

"A very productive day," he was saying to Miss Clemency. "My fieldwork has yielded gratifying results, and I am pleased to say I will shortly be able to add several new species to the *Caryophyllaceae* family."

Mother had never tolerated Father's talk about plants. But Miss Clemency nodded eagerly, and, talking with her, Father looked happy.

But I couldn't feel happy for him.

I didn't know that my father had had a sister. He had never told me. He never told me anything. Never paid any attention to me. Hardly noticed me at all.

Suddenly, everything about Father—the way he was talking, the way he was waving his fork about—made me angry. I had never felt anger like this before. It rolled over me like a wave. It left my knees wobbling and knocked the breath out of my lungs.

Before I could think about what I was doing, I slammed my knife against my plate. Hard. Cabbage stew spattered the table-top, and the ringing sound of silver on china made everyone around the table jump.

Father placed his own fork, quite deliberately, next to his plate and looked up at me.

He had noticed me now.

Miss Clemency had, too. And, from her darkened corner, even Mrs. Purswell was staring.

They looked at me expectantly, like they were waiting for me to say something.

I turned to Zenobia, feeling panicked. Now that I had Father's attention, I didn't know what to do with it.

"Go on," she said. Her voice was almost gentle. "Ask him."

"Tell me about Tourmaline," I said. My voice came out louder than I expected it to.

Father didn't ask me to repeat myself and he didn't lean for-ward in his chair to hear me better.

"Not now, Elizabeth," he said.

"Not now," I asked, "or not ever?"

"I *said*, not now."

"I may be speaking out of turn, Dr. Murmur," said Miss

Clemency, and her cheeks glowed red, "but surely Elizabeth has a right to know . . ."

She trailed off and looked intently at her cabbage stew.

"Tourmaline. My sister." Father's voice caught on the word "sister." "She . . . she's not with us anymore."

"But—"

"No more questions. You asked me about Tourmaline. I have told you about Tourmaline. It all happened a long time ago. I don't wish to discuss it any further."

"But—"

He stood up, pushing back his chair so violently that it tipped over and fell to the floor. "Enough, Elizabeth!" he roared. "That is *enough*!"

He strode past me and out of the room.

As he went by my chair, I saw that his eyes were glistening. I think they might have been filling with tears.

Miss Clemency reached across the table and laid her hand over mine. "Tourmaline must have been very dear to him," she said gently.

I studied my fingernails. They were still black with dirt from the graveyard. "I don't think *anyone's* ever been very dear to him," I muttered.

"I'm sure that's not true," Miss Clemency said softly. She looked like she might say more, but I gave her such a dark look that she fell silent. Finally, she gave a delicate yawn and said,

"My, it *has* been a long day, hasn't it? Perhaps you'd let me walk you up to your bedroom, Elizabeth?"

I shook my head. "I think I'll stay here a little longer," I said.

"Just a little longer, then." Miss Clemency squeezed my shoulder as she went past me and out of the room.

I turned to Zenobia. "I don't understand," I said in a dull voice. "Why would Father keep such a secret?"

"It's all quite shrouded in mystery, isn't it?" said Zenobia. "The long-hidden sister. The overgrown grave." A grin crept into the corners of her mouth. "I do love a good mystery."

"But I don't!" I snapped. "And I don't want Tourmaline to be a mystery, either! She would have been my aunt, if she had lived. And I don't know anything about her. I don't even know what she looked like!"

I heard a throat-clearing sound near my elbow. Mrs. Purswell had materialized. She gave me a strange look—almost a pitying look, I thought.

"Uncanny," breathed Zenobia.

But while Zenobia was impressed, I was embarrassed. It must have looked to Mrs. Purswell as though I was talking to myself.

Mrs. Purswell stacked the cabbage-smeared dishes and went to disappear again. Then she turned around. She looked like she was about to say something. Whatever it was, though, she thought better of it. She pressed her lips together and melted into the darkness.

———◆———

In the blue guest bedroom, I sat at the window seat with my breath misting the glass. Through the window was the moon. When we first arrived at Witheringe House, it was the shape of a fingernail clipping. Now it was round, nearly full, and tinged yellow. We had been almost a fortnight here.

Any hopes I had that things would improve between Father and me at the new house were gone.

I sighed.

I was still angry, though not in the way I had been angry at dinner. Now I was a mixture of angry and confused and hurt.

Zenobia sprang onto the seat with me. I pulled my knees up to make room for her. She didn't talk. She just softly opened her book. But I could tell that she meant, in her own way, to comfort me. I leaned against her and felt her cold closeness.

I knew Tourmaline would stay a mystery to me. Father would never speak of her again—he had made that much clear. I wished I could put her from my mind.

With a rustle, Zenobia turned her page. My eye fell on the sentence she was reading.

> *. . . but when we call up a Spirit Presence, we do not call up that Presence alone: a Spirit Presence brings with it the Keys to the Past, and to all the Long-Forgotten Secrets, Mysteries, and Memories that lie within it . . .*

I sat up straight.

If Father wouldn't tell me about Tourmaline, then maybe *Tourmaline* would tell me about Tourmaline.

"Zenobia?"

Zenobia let her book fall shut. "Yes?"

"Do you think Witheringe House is haunted?"

"*Inhabited*, Elizabeth, not haunted. Inhabited by a Spirit Presence."

"And do you think the Spirit Presence inhabits the nursery?"

"So my senses tell me."

"Then do you think there's a possibility that the Spirit Presence in the nursery might be Tourmaline?"

Zenobia's eyes shone. "Why do you ask?" she said.

I bit my lip. I knew what I wanted to say next. I knew, too, that once I said it, there would be no taking it back.

The words rushed out. "Because I want to talk with her," I said. And as soon as I had said the words, I knew them to be true. For all that I was scared of ghosts and séances, I wanted to talk to Tourmaline very much.

Zenobia smiled widely. "But that's a marvelous idea, Elizabeth! So marvelous, I wonder why I didn't think of it myself! We'll hold another séance. And we'll address Tourmaline directly." Her eyes were bright. "Tourmaline," she said, testing it out. Liking the sound of it, she said it again. "Tourmaline." Then she went on, "Madame Lucent says if you call a Spirit Presence by its True Name, it's far more likely to answer you. Or at least, I think that's what she says."

I sprang down from the window seat. I found one sock and I started to hunt around for its pair.

"Now, which chapter was it?" The pages of the book ruffled against the tips of Zenobia's fingers. "Let me see. 'Spirit Doubles and How to Find Yours'—no. 'Ten Types of Visitation'—no."

I found the other sock, and I began to push my feet into my shoes.

"Here it is!" she said, and she started to read.

> *"Though the Spectral Inhabitants of the World Beyond the Veil have shed their fleshly forms, they are yet bound to the World of the Living through the names by which they were called. Call a Spirit Presence by its True Name once more and even the most reluctant may be compelled to Answer you."*

"Well," I said, putting my arms through the sleeves of my jacket, "that sounds very promising."

"Now," said Zenobia, "when would you like to hold the séance? We could wait until midnight. I always think midnight is the most atmospheric time. Or"—her eye caught the moon through the window—"we could wait a few more days until the moon is full. We wouldn't need the candle. We could conduct the whole séance by the moon's eerie light."

When she looked back from the window, I was standing, fully clothed, at the door, and fitting the candle into its silver holder.

"Now," I said. "I want to have the séance now."

Zenobia looked at me admiringly. "You're a different Elizabeth altogether from the one you were this afternoon." She grinned. "I like it."

Zenobia tucked a book of matches into her pocket, and slowly, so that its creaking wouldn't wake the sleeping house, she opened the door.

By the time we got to the nursery, I was starting to feel more like the old Elizabeth. The one who was timid and afraid of ghosts and darkness. The one who wondered if this séance was such a good idea after all.

Zenobia opened the door a crack. "Come on," she said.

My voice shook. "I don't know if I can, after all," I said. "I'm not brave like you."

"I'm *not* brave," she said. "I'm just not scared. There's a difference."

"There is?" I asked.

"Do you know what's brave, Elizabeth? When you're scared to do something, but you do it anyway."

She pushed the door open wide and went into the nursery.

I decided, just for tonight, I would be brave. I followed her.

The bright moon shone through the window. The mirror on the wall showed its reflection, tinged green and rippled, in its murky glass.

Perhaps it was the moonlight that made the green nursery wallpaper somehow even brighter and greener than before. The tree that grew across one wall seemed taller. The two branches that grew from each side of its trunk looked almost like arms, and they twisted and split apart at their ends to make shapes like open hands with reaching twiggy fingers.

I turned my back to the tree.

Zenobia lit the candle. She threaded the ring onto its twine. Then she laid out the Ouija board and sat cross-legged before it.

"Are you ready?" She looked up at me.

"I'm ready," I said. I took my place on the other side of the board.

Zenobia opened Madame Lucent's book.

"O Spirit," she began in a loud, ringing voice.

I cleared my throat. "Zenobia?"

"Don't interrupt," she whispered. She closed her eyes and tipped her face to the ceiling. "O Spirit," she boomed.

"But, Zenobia."

"*What?*" She snapped her eyes open and gave me an annoyed look.

"Well, we didn't decide before the séance who should be the one to ask the questions."

"*I* am always the one to ask the questions, Elizabeth. *I* am the medium. *I* bring a certain gravity to the role that, frankly, I'm not sure you're capable of."

"I just thought that I might ask the questions this time."

Tourmaline was, after all, my father's sister. And had she lived, she would have been my aunt. Surely she belonged to me more than to Zenobia.

"No one *owns* a Spirit Presence, Elizabeth," Zenobia broke in on my thoughts. "And I do have a finer understanding of the art of mediumship, not that I like to point it out—"

"You do, though," I said. "You do like to point it out. You just pointed it out now."

Zenobia leaned in close and spoke in a hiss so pronounced, the candle between us flickered and nearly went out.

"Well, if you're at all as attuned to the Spirit World," she said, "you'll know that bickering isn't conducive to communication with Spirit Visitors. Now"—she allowed a serene expression to fall over her face—"kindly put your fingers to the corners of the board and follow my lead."

I did as I was told.

In a voice that was soft and solemn, Zenobia addressed her questions to Tourmaline, reading from the book.

"O Tourmaline, what Troubles have you Seen?

"O Tourmaline, what Impels you to Wander these Halls?

"O Tourmaline, do you have a Message of Great Importance for us?"

Each question was answered with silence. The ring stayed motionless in the air.

I peered at Zenobia over the candle.

"Fine, then," snapped Zenobia. "If you think you can do better—"

"I never said I thought I could do *better*—"

"You didn't need to," said Zenobia. "Here." She passed me the book.

"Actually," I said, "I thought I might ask my own questions."

"These are the questions that Madame Lucent specifically recommends. Madame Lucent, may I remind you, is a Famed and Celebrated Clairvoyant with over forty years' experience in dealing with the World Beyond the Veil."

"I know that, but—"

Zenobia raised an eyebrow at me. "Perhaps you are also a Famed and Celebrated Clairvoyant?"

"You know I'm not, but . . . but these questions are all wrong!" I burst out. "Please, let me talk to her in my own way."

"Oh, fine, then," Zenobia relented. "One question."

I let my mind go blank. When I opened my mouth, the words flowed. "Tourmaline," I said, "I'm Elizabeth. And I'd like to talk to you, if you'd like to talk to me. You see, you're very special to someone who is very special to me. And this person is very sad to have lost you but . . . but he won't tell me any more than that. And I need to know more. So I was hoping that you might tell me. What happened to you, Tourmaline?"

In the silence that followed my question, I looked at the ring. It stayed perfectly still.

But the candle guttered. Long, dark shadows spilled over the nursery's walls. And the wallpaper seemed to *move*, only for an instant. But in that instant, I saw the plants and trees rustling and swaying, as if bent by a strong wind. And I saw shadowy, leafy figures that moved like people among the plants. The mirror turned murky. The dark green shapes reflected in its glass were not shapes I could find anywhere in the room.

My skin prickled.

And then the candle flame glowed steady again. The wallpaper was still. And the mirror showed the nursery—the rocking horse, the cots, the Ouija board—once more.

I leaned across the Ouija board. "Did you feel that?" I asked.

"Feel what, exactly?" asked Zenobia.

I stared at her in confusion. "Why, Tourmaline," I said. "She was all around us."

"Elizabeth, be serious," Zenobia snapped.

"Are you saying you didn't see the wallpaper? It was moving!"

"I am *trying* to make contact with the world Beyond the Veil, Elizabeth. I am trying to speak with a Spirit Presence. I won't be distracted from my purpose by . . . by wallpaper."

"B–But," I sputtered. I had no way of proving that what I had just seen was real. Still, I felt at the very bottom of my stomach that *something* had happened. Something important. I searched for the words to explain this feeling to Zenobia, but they didn't come.

"Now," she said, "if you'll kindly hand the book back to me, we can continue the séance *properly*."

It was late in the night now—perhaps even early in the morning—and our candle had burned down to a pool of wax. Zenobia had asked every question in Madame Lucent's book. Some she had even asked twice.

None of the questions had received a response. But I remembered how the wallpaper had sprung to life and the feeling that Tourmaline was nearer than ever before, and I didn't lose hope.

Zenobia clapped her book shut.

"That's it," she said. "I've had enough."

"You can't give up!"

"I should have given up a long time ago," she said. "I've followed Madame Lucent's instructions to the letter, and I'm no closer to making contact with a Spirit Presence than I was when I first arrived at Witheringe House."

"But it's not just some Spirit Presence we're trying to make contact with now. It's Tourmaline. And I know she's here, Zenobia. If we can just find the right question—if we can just ask it in the right way."

Zenobia shook her head firmly. "This"—she waved the book in front of my face—"is a waste of my time." And she hurled the book into a corner of the nursery. "All my efforts trying to contact a Spirit Presence," she said bitterly, "when I could have been learning hieroglyphics, or refining my telekinesis technique— doing something *useful*!"

My insides turned cold. This was how it always was with Zenobia. One day, she'd spend hours poring over the shape of tea leaves at the bottom of an empty cup, wondering what message they held for her. The next day, she'd tire of tasseomancy—she'd move on to taxidermy, or necromancy. And she would never try to read a fortune in a teacup again.

Normally, I didn't mind. Normally, I was even relieved when Zenobia finished with one of her phases. After all, they usually became tiresome to me far sooner than they became tiresome to her. But if Zenobia was giving up on clairvoyance, she wasn't just giving up on Madame Lucent. She was giving up on Tourmaline. And it felt, in a small way, that she was giving up on me.

"But what about Tourmaline?" I pleaded. "What about the Spirit Presence you felt in this room?"

Zenobia got to her feet and stalked over to the door. "Some-times spooky old rooms are just that, Elizabeth—spooky old rooms. I'm going to bed."

The door clicked shut behind her.

I stayed where I was. I felt numb.

Slowly, I gathered up the Ouija board, the melted candle, and the silver ring.

The World Beyond: One Famed and Celebrated Clairvoyant's Guide to the World of the Spirits lay splayed open in the corner where Zenobia had flung it. I bent to retrieve it. But halfway to the floor, I stopped. I stared. A pair of wide eyes stared back at me.

The wallpaper girl.

She was crouched just above the wainscoting in the corner, by a bush covered in flowers with petals that were long and curved and sharp-looking, like swords. Her hand was stretched out as if to pluck one of the spiky flowers before her.

But the last time I had seen her, she had been by the window-sill. Hadn't she?

I brought the candle to the window. I looked all around its sill. There was no wallpaper girl there.

I went back to the corner. There she was, with a ribbon com-ing loose in her wild, tangled hair and the striped fabric of her pinafore bunched at her knees.

I must have misremembered, then, where I had seen her last.

I tucked the book under my arm. With my hand on the door-knob, I stopped and looked back at the nursery. The two narrow cots against the wall. The bookshelf filled with fairy tales. The dappled gray rocking horse that shone silver in the moonlight. The wallpaper girl in her far, dark corner.

Yes, I must have misremembered her place in the wallpaper.

8

The Nursery

id you know, Elizabeth, that the chief ingredient in green dye was once arsenic?"

"No," I said, "I guess I didn't." I poured milk into my cup and blinked sleepily at the white cloud it made over the surface of my tea. I hadn't slept last night. Every time I had closed my eyes, I'd seen the bright green wallpaper of the nursery and the vines and the plants and the twisted tree that covered it.

"Of course," she said, "arsenic is deadly poisonous."

Zenobia was reading a large blue book. Its title was embossed in gold letters. *The Poisoner's Alphabet: An Amateur's Guide to Common Toxins and Their Dreadful Effects.*

Clearly, she hadn't read past "A."

"It was arsenic green," she said, "that was used to dye the silk for emerald ball gowns. More than one young girl came home after a night of dancing in her bright green dress and dropped down dead!"

"Where did you find that book?"

"I happened upon it in the library."

"So you're not reading *The World Beyond* anymore?"

"As I said last night," Zenobia explained, "Madame Lucent has, regrettably, overstated her knowledge of the Spirit World. I haven't lifted the Veil to the World Beyond. I'm starting to think Madame Lucent hasn't, either. So, I've given up on clairvoyance, at least for the time being." She looked, briefly, disappointed. Then she brightened. "I'm all about toxicology now. Toxicology," she said, in answer to the question that formed in my mind, "is the study of poisons. One never knows when a knowledge of deadly substances might prove useful."

"No," I said sadly, "I suppose one doesn't."

So Zenobia really had given up. Perhaps she was right to. It had been foolish of me to think we might have contacted Tourmaline. And even if we could have—what would be the point? Tourmaline was long dead, and whatever I did, she was going to stay that way.

I sipped my tea and grimaced. It was cold.

"Excuse me, Miss Elizabeth?" Mrs. Purswell appeared at my elbow and raised an eyebrow in the direction of my breakfast. "May I take your plate?"

I nodded. "Thank you, Mrs. Purswell."

She balanced my teacup and saucer on the plate and lifted them from the table. I waited for her to ooze back into the shadows.

But she stayed where she was. She reached a hand into her apron pocket and then placed a square of paper on the table before me.

I looked down at the paper for just long enough to see that it was a photograph.

When I looked up, Mrs. Purswell was gone.

I held the photograph in my hands. It must have been crisp once, but it was faded sepia now and creased and crinkled at its edges.

It showed a boy sitting in a stiff-backed chair. He held a butterfly net in his hands, and he looked into the camera with a serious expression. Beside him stood a girl, resting her hand against the back of the chair. She wore a lace dress, and her short hair was curled into ringlets. She was smaller than the boy and blurred around her edges, as if she hadn't been able to stay still long enough for the camera to capture her. But her face was clear enough. She had a wide smile. More of a grin than a smile, I thought, tracing its curve with my little finger. A freckle on her left cheek had almost the same shape as a heart.

I turned the photograph over to see, written in copperplate, *Henry aged nine, Tourmaline aged seven.*

Tourmaline. I sucked in my breath and drew the photograph close to my face. I studied Tourmaline.

There was something about her—her face, or her eyes, or the way she seemed to move even as she stood still—that made me feel I had seen her before. Perhaps, I decided, I recognized in her some family resemblance.

I went to pass the photograph to Zenobia, who was absorbed in *The Poisoner's Alphabet*. But something stopped me.

I remembered the way the wallpaper had moved in the nursery last night, the ghostly presence I had felt all around me. And I remembered how Zenobia had dismissed it all as if it was nothing.

I slipped the photograph into my pocket.

I would find Tourmaline, I thought to myself, without Zenobia's help.

Miss Clemency's hand flew across the blackboard. A blue-chalk Pacific Ocean appeared beneath her fingers. She clapped the chalk dust from her hands and opened her geography book.

"I have been very much looking forward to this lesson," she announced, "for in it we learn about the deepest, darkest, most mysterious part of the ocean: the Mariana Trench."

The Mariana Trench, Miss Clemency explained, is a deep ditch in the ocean floor—so deep, no one knows how deep it truly is.

I tried to keep my thoughts anchored there, to the very bottom of the ocean floor. But no matter how hard I tried, they always floated away. To the nursery. To Tourmaline.

"And just think, Elizabeth!" The sound of my name pulled me back into the classroom. "There's no light at the bottom of the Mariana Trench. It's so dark that all the fishes who live there sprout cunning little lanterns out of the tops of their heads, to light the way before them. Doesn't that sound festive?"

"Oh, yes," I agreed in a dull voice. "Very festive."

Miss Clemency closed her book. "You seem very far away this lesson," she said, and she pulled her chair close to mine. "I know the last few days haven't been easy for you. Is there something you'd like to talk about, Elizabeth?"

I looked into Miss Clemency's kind, questioning face. I wanted to tell her everything. About the strange wallpaper and the blurry girl in the photograph and the hurt I felt when I saw Zenobia hunched over *The Poisoner's Alphabet*, absorbed in the entry for belladonna, with her back turned to me. But how could I tell it to her in a way that made sense?

I stared at my hands and said nothing.

"I think you have a lot on your mind," she said.

I nodded.

"When I have a lot on my mind," she continued, "I find there's only one reliable remedy. Poetry."

"Poetry?" I asked doubtfully.

She gave a firm nod. "Poetry. Tell me, Elizabeth, have you ever learned a poem by heart?"

I shook my head.

"When your heart is beating too quick with nerves, there's nothing like the rhythm of a poem to bring it right again. When you fill your mind up with words—beautiful words, stirring words—those words drive away your other worries."

I thought guiltily of Tourmaline. "But I don't *want* to just forget my worries," I said. "Not entirely."

"Of course not," said Miss Clemency. "But if you're to tackle those worries, you'll need a clear, calm mind. I think we should come back to geography another day. For now . . ." She stood on tiptoe and brought down a heavy volume of poetry from a shelf. She riffled through its pages.

"Wordsworth?" she muttered. "Hmm. Byron? Best not. Aha!" She laid the book open on the table in front of me.

"'The Lady of Shalott,'" I read, "by Alfred, Lord Tennyson."

"It's a beautiful poem," Miss Clemency said. "Melancholic and suspenseful. And the words! The words are like a current you can float away on! It's a poem about a girl who lives under a fairy curse, until—" She stopped. A small secret smile pulled at the corners of her mouth. "Well, perhaps I shan't tell you—you'll find it all out for yourself."

I bent my head over the book and read the first stanza.

> *On either side the river lie*
> *Long fields of barley and of rye,*
> *That clothe the wold and meet the sky;*
> *And thro' the field the road runs by*
> *To many-tower'd Camelot*

Miss Clemency was right. Reading the poem, letting its words fill my ears and my mind, calmed me. I read it over and over, until our lesson ended.

Later, in the blue guest bedroom, I lifted the mattress a little and eased the sepia photograph underneath it. Then, sitting propped against the pillows, I opened the book again. I was in Witheringe House still, but in my mind, I was with the Lady of Shalott in her island castle.

> *The little isle is all inrail'd,*
> *With a rose-fence, and overtrail'd,*
> *With roses: by the marge unhail'd*

Filling my head with poetry stopped my thoughts circling around Tourmaline. I was thinking about the Lady instead, imprisoned in her room, away from the world. I was thinking about the words—*isle, overtrail'd*—and how well they sat in my ears.

> *The shallop flitteth silken sail'd,*
> *Skimming down to Camelot.*

A shallop, I thought, was a type of boat. Zenobia looked up from *The Poisoner's Alphabet*, in which she had been studying an illustration of a sharp-leafed plant, and fixed me with a withering stare. "How am I ever to learn the difference between common hemlock and poison hemlock with you muttering away about boats?"

"Miss Clemency set me a poem to learn. I think you'd like it, Zenobia. It's 'The Lady of Shalott.' It's all about a girl who lives in the turret of a beautiful island castle—"

Zenobia gave an exaggerated yawn.

"And she's under a terrible curse."

Zenobia brightened. "Oh?"

"She's not allowed to look out her window. She can only see the world through the mirror above her bed. But one day, a knight rides past the castle. He sings so beautifully that she rushes to the window to see him—"

"And does it end badly?" asked Zenobia greedily.

"Oh, yes, very badly."

"*How* badly?"

"With her pale corpse floating on a raft down the river to Camelot."

"Well, that part does sound agreeable."

"I already know it almost all by heart," I said, and I passed her the book. "And besides, it's late." I turned over and closed my eyes, ready for sleep.

But later, I woke up. Moonlight streamed through the window. It was too bright to sleep. I looked around for a book to read. Zenobia had fallen asleep over the Tennyson, and I couldn't pull it out from under her head without waking her. I reached instead for *The Plant Kingdom* by Dr. Henry Murmur.

I read about rushes and dillweed until my eyes fell slowly closed. I put the book away and turned to go to sleep. As I did, my eyes caught on the clock. Eleven fifty-nine.

I wondered.

I took the book and opened it on my lap again. And I waited for the stroke of midnight.

When the clock chimed, I turned the page. And there were the looping green letters.

After the little Prince died, the Plant Kingdom fell into mourning. The leaves on the trees turned dry and brown. The grass wilted. The flowers were too sad to bloom and the insects too mournful to buzz or fly or bite. Saddest of all was the Queen. Every day she sank her roots into the earth under a bare tree in the palace gardens and cried. After many days her tears made a deep, silver pool. And still the Queen cried, and the pool grew deeper and more silver.

At the bottom of the pool, the Queen saw strange things. Things like she had never seen before. A gauzy white net. A wooden horse. And, one day, a girl. The girl was so joyful that, looking at her, the Queen almost forgot she was sad.

She called the King, and the King and Queen watched the girl playing with the white gauzy net, lifting it over her head and swooping it through the air, laughing. The King and Queen wondered what it would be like if the little girl was theirs. They thought that if they could have the girl, even for a short time, they wouldn't feel so sad. They might not feel sad at all.

Perhaps, they thought, they could borrow the girl. Just for a little while.

I was fast asleep when I felt the blanket slipping off me. I fumbled it back over myself.

The blanket jerked away. I yanked it back.

Then the blanket was gone and cold air washed over me.

My eyes snapped open. The blanket was levitating three inches above me. Zenobia stood by the bed, muttering and staring intently at the floating blanket. I snatched it out of the air, wrapped it, shawl-like, around me, and swung my legs over the side of the bed.

"I was *sleeping*," I told her.

"Which is precisely why I was forced to wake you up."

"It's *Saturday*."

"It certainly is. You have no lessons. Your father has locked himself in his study and he won't be out for hours. Mrs. Purswell's gone into Witheringe Green for groceries, and Miss Clemency has accompanied her—I believe she's buying hat ribbon or some other equally ghastly thing. So there is no one to disturb us."

I rubbed the sleep from my eyes. "No one to disturb us doing what? And why are you dressed like that?"

Zenobia wore her tinted glasses and carried her black silk parasol.

"Because the sun's out," she said, "which is a shame, though it can't be helped." She narrowed her eyes and scowled out the window as if she might scare the sun out of the sky, but it stayed where it was, shining and round. "In all other respects, however, it's a fine day for hunting mushrooms."

"Mushrooms?"

Zenobia opened *The Poisoner's Alphabet* and read.

"While many mushroom varietals are harmless, others, such as the death-cap mushroom (Amanita phalloides) *secrete deadly amounts of poison invisible to the untrained eye."*

"Why would you want to go looking for poisonous mushrooms?" I asked, with my mouth foaming with toothpaste. And then my insides turned heavy and cold. I spat into the basin and whipped around. "Zenobia, you don't mean to—"

"I'm not going to *poison* anyone," she snapped. "I'm a poison enthusiast, Elizabeth, not a poisoner—a fine, yet vital, distinction. I simply think it would be thrilling to find a specimen of the deadly *Amanita phalloides,* to come so close to something so fatal. Don't you?"

Rather than answer the question, I bent over my shoes.

"Hurry up," said Zenobia. "*The Poisoner's Alphabet* clearly states that the best time to look for death caps is morning."

I didn't want to spend Saturday in the garden. I had planned to comb the house for clues that might lead me to Tourmaline. But an idea was starting to form in my head. A morning in the garden, I thought, might not be a waste of time after all.

I fumbled with my shoelaces. "You go ahead," I said. "I'll catch up with you."

After Zenobia left the room, I felt under the mattress for where I had hidden the photograph of Tourmaline. I slipped it into my pocket.

———◆———

Outside, I shivered. The ground was damp and dewy and its coldness came up through the soles of my shoes. Zenobia stalked ahead of me, making for the sundial.

Halfway there, she crouched. "Elizabeth!" she called back over her shoulder.

I came and looked at the place where she had parted the long grass with her hands.

"Aren't they beautiful?" she breathed.

Truthfully, I didn't like the look of them. I much preferred the common toadstool, with its cheery red cap and white spots. These were small and glowering. Their pointed caps had the same color and shine as a bruise faded to green. Zenobia poked one until it bent over and showed its inky underfrilling.

"They're very . . . singular looking," I said at last.

"Singular," said Zenobia, enthralled. "Yes, that's exactly the word for them."

My fingers touched the photograph in my pocket. I wanted more than ever to find out about Tourmaline. I intended to go back to the nursery to talk to the gardener. And I meant to go back alone.

I straightened up. "I think I see another patch over there," I lied.

"Over where?"

I looked around desperately for a landmark. "Over there by

the . . . by the hedge maze. Perhaps I should go and take a closer look?"

"Yes," she said. "You might look inside the maze, too. According to *The Poisoner's Alphabet*, death caps grow best in patches of dark shade."

"I'll be sure to look, then," I lied again.

I made my way toward the maze. I could feel Zenobia's eyes on me, watching as I went.

Zenobia was still watching me when I reached the hedge maze. Would she ever take her eyes off me?

Before I knew it, I had given her a small wave and stepped inside.

I had only taken a few shallow steps before the entrance was obscured. All I could see around me was the dark, choking maze and the bare, spiky branches of the dead tree at its center, reaching out over the hedges. The thump of my heart pounded in my ears. What if I *did* get lost? What if I couldn't find my way out again? What if no one came looking for me?

I needed to get out. I started back the way I had come, but every turn I took only seemed to lead me farther into the maze.

I breathed deeply to stop my rising panic.

Finally, a shaft of sunlight fell across my path. I was at the maze's entrance. I ventured a peek at Zenobia.

Her eyes were fixed on the ground.

Here was my chance.

I crept out of the maze, resolving never to go in there again. I dashed up the hill, slipping from tree to tree so Zenobia wouldn't see me. I edged along the crest until I came to the moss-covered nursery shed.

I opened the door.

Weaving through trellises and past flower beds, I made my way to the worktable. It was covered, as before, with saplings and clods of soil and heavy garden tools. I picked up a pair of shears and felt the weight of them in my hands.

I looked around. There was no one there but me.

Perhaps Father was right and I had just imagined—

"Be careful with those," came a soft, light voice. "You could lose a finger. Or more."

I dropped the shears onto the table, filled with relief. I hadn't imagined the gardener after all. He stood there, real as could be, brushing crumbs of dirt from his waistcoat with his gloved hands.

"I'm glad to see you again," I said. "I remember you said you'd worked at Witheringe House a long time. And so I thought you'd be the best person to ask."

"To ask about what?"

I took the photograph from my pocket and placed it on the table.

The gardener's smile pulled down into a grim line. He jerked the shears away from me and began to sharpen them against a whetstone. The blades of the shears made bright, loud sparks where they ground against the stone.

"I don't have time to talk today," he said over the noise of the shears and the stone. "I'm very busy."

Odd. He hadn't seemed busy. "Busy with what?" I asked.

The gardener tested the sharpness of the shears against his gloved thumb. He seemed satisfied. Then he brought the jaws of the shears together around a sapling. It snipped easily in half, and its sap spilled over the table.

"Busy with grafting," he said at last. He pointed to a flower bed. Growing there was the plant with the pale pink flowers. I looked at it and saw how the cultivar had bent and twisted around the rootstock. Already there were places where the rootstock and cultivar were tangled so tightly together, they were more like one plant than two. The new plant was still covered in leaves, and its flowers still smelled like powdered sugar, but there was something nasty and misshapen about it.

The plant with pale pink flowers wasn't the only one in the flower bed. Since I had last been in the nursery, it seemed the gardener had been busy grafting. He had chosen strange-looking plants to graft—plants I had never seen in any garden before. One had a layer of soft, silky fur growing over its leaves. Another was covered in blossoms of a color somewhere between yellow and orange that I was sure didn't have a name.

The gardener stood behind me. "They're very fine, aren't they?" He sounded pleased. Proud, even.

"Yes," I said, though I didn't think the poor twisted plants looked fine at all. They looked *wrong*.

"And if you think *these* are fine"—he stopped and cleared his throat—"but I shouldn't say."

"Shouldn't say what?" I moved down the length of the flower bed and stopped to inspect the last plant. Its rootstock was a swarthy shrub nearly bare of leaves. Grafted to it with twine was a plant covered with mauve flowers. Their petals were long and curved and sharp-looking, like sword blades.

"All this," he said, and he waved a hand over the plants, "is just practice. Soon, I shall graft something very special."

In between the mauve sword-blade flowers, I saw a flash of red. I reached in through the branches and pulled out a small red shoe. When I touched it, a strange shiver prickled through me. I couldn't say whether it was a shiver of fear or of something else. Maybe this was what Zenobia meant by a *frisson*.

"It will be a grafting like none that has ever been attempted before," said the gardener.

I looked closer at the shoe. It was made from leather, and it fastened at one side with a brass buckle.

"Whose shoe is this?" I asked the gardener.

His eyes narrowed. "No one's," he snapped. "Now come away from there. These plants are very delicate."

I stayed where I was, frowning at the shoe in my hand.

The gardener's voice turned crafty and coaxing. "If you come away from there, Miss Elizabeth, I'll tell you everything you want to know about Tourmaline." He beckoned for me to join him at the other side of the worktable.

And I did join him. But not before I stuffed the red shoe into my pocket.

The gardener peered at the photograph. When he looked up, he said, "The truth about Tourmaline is that she disappeared."

"People don't simply disappear," I said.

"Tourmaline did. It was a fine day, the day she vanished. She was playing in the garden with Henry. Henry, it seems, spied a butterfly—a fritillary butterfly, quite uncommon at that time of year—and wanted a closer look. Tourmaline ran to fetch his butterfly net. And she never came back."

"What happened to her?"

"No one knows. She was nowhere to be found. They turned the house inside out looking for her. The whole village scoured the hills and fields for a sign of her. But there was none. It's as I said. She disappeared."

"It doesn't make any sense," I said. "She must have gone *somewhere*." I reached for the photograph, but the gardener lifted it out of my grasp. He turned his wide smile on me, but this time I didn't find it kind at all.

"Wherever Tourmaline is," he said, "she's very well hidden. So well hidden, she'll never be found." He pressed the photograph back into my hands.

"I should leave you to your work, I think," I said.

"Good-bye for now, then," said the gardener. His smile turned wider. "But it won't be too long, I think, before I see you again, Miss Elizabeth."

"That would be nice," I said, and I hoped he couldn't tell that I wasn't telling the truth.

I stood outside the nursery shed. Sunlight fell on the photograph, right across Tourmaline's face.

I felt my blood stop in my veins.

I knew where I had seen her before.

I looked at Zenobia, farther down the hill, still bent over her toadstools. She would notice soon that I had taken too long coming back. But I would worry about her later.

I hurried down through the orchard. I went into the house through the kitchen, through the cool, floury larder and past the blazing stove, and up the stairs into the front room. I went to the tapestry. I felt the weight of it in my hand. And I pushed it aside.

9

The Wallpaper Girl

In the nursery, I tore open the curtains. As soon as the sunlight came in, I was dazzled by the wallpaper. Its green was so bright, I couldn't look straight at it without my eyes shifting and sliding around. It felt to me that the plants and vines in the pattern were shifting and sliding around, too. Squinting the green away, I went to the place above the wain-scoting where I had seen the wallpaper girl last.

She wasn't there.

I turned in a slow circle. I didn't see the girl. But I did see the tree that covered most of one wall. It had grown, I thought, even bigger since the last time I saw it. Now it branched out over the walls and crept up over the ceiling. A tangled beard of lichen sprouted from its trunk, and two deep knots were set, like eyes, into its rough bark. Over the knots that looked like eyes, dark, spiky leaves twisted in the shape of a crown.

A shiver needled down my spine. Looking at it, I knew the tree was more than just a tree. I knew it was the Plant King.

I searched the wallpaper again, inch by inch. At last, I found the wallpaper girl beneath the murky mirror. I held the photograph of Tourmaline up close to her face. Tourmaline's hair was coaxed into ringlets, and the wallpaper girl's was bushy and wild. Tourmaline's dress was spotless, and the wallpaper girl's was stained and rumpled. Tourmaline had a heart-shaped freckle on her left cheek, and the wallpaper girl had a heart-shaped freckle on her right cheek.

But the two girls were, in every other way, exactly the same.

I brushed my fingers softly over the wallpaper girl.

"Tourmaline," I whispered.

And then I looked down at her feet. I saw that she wore, on her left foot, a red shoe, fastened with a brass buckle.

Her right foot was bare.

I looked at the small red shoe I had found in the plant nursery. I didn't need to check it against the shoe the wallpaper girl wore to know the two shoes were a pair.

I had wanted to find out what happened to Tourmaline without Zenobia's help. But that was before I had matched the girl in the photograph with the girl in the wallpaper, and the red shoe from the nursery with the red shoe in the wallpaper.

Now I needed to tell Zenobia what I had found.

I looked for her all through the house, and when she wasn't in the house, I looked for her all over the garden. But I didn't see her for the rest of the day. Mrs. Purswell laid a plate for her at dinner. I looked at it guiltily. I knew Zenobia was angry. Because while she sometimes went off and left *me* alone, I had never gone off and left *her*. Not until now.

I found her at last in the blue guest bedroom, cultivating a small colony of *Amanita phalloides* in a gap between the floorboards.

"I've been wondering where you were," I said.

"I might say the same for you," came the icy reply.

"I can explain. There was something I had to do."

This was met with chill silence.

"If you would let me explain, I'm sure you wouldn't be so angry."

Zenobia pretended she hadn't heard. She bent lower over her death-cap mushrooms.

"It's important, what I have to tell you," I said. "I've found something out. About Tourmaline."

Still, Zenobia said nothing.

I sighed and flopped down on the bed. I reached for "The Lady of Shalott" to calm my mind, but I found I couldn't concentrate on it.

I was angry at Zenobia. I didn't think I deserved this silent treatment. But I felt like I might burst if I didn't tell someone about Tourmaline—and soon.

In the end, my impatience to tell her what I had discovered won out.

"Zenobia?" I said.

She ignored me.

"Zenobia, I'm sorry," I said.

Her ears pricked up and she turned to face me.

"I shouldn't have left you on your own," I continued. "I hope you'll forgive me when I tell you why I did."

"Well"—she tamped the last of the soil around the death-cap stems and brushed dirt crumbs from her fingers—"retrospectively, I may have overreacted to your going off like that, and I'm . . ." She paused for an uncomfortably long time.

"Yes?"

"I'm . . . I'm regretful."

"Regretful?"

"I'm penitent. I'm contrite. I'm—"

"Zenobia, are you trying to tell me you're sorry, too?"

"If that's how you want to interpret it, I can't stop you. Now, tell me, what have you found out? Is it something very gruesome?"

I explained everything. I started with the book that told the story of the Plant Kingdom and the girl in the nursery wallpaper. I showed Zenobia the photograph that Mrs. Purswell had given me and told her how the girl in the wallpaper matched almost exactly the photograph of Tourmaline. I told her what the gardener had told me, that Tourmaline had just disappeared one day, and no trace of her had ever been found. I showed her the red shoe I had found in the nursery, and told her about the red shoe that was missing from the wallpaper girl's right foot.

And then, nervously, I explained how I thought the wallpaper in the nursery showed the Plant Kingdom—that the Plant Kingdom, somehow, existed in the nursery wallpaper. And that although I didn't know how, exactly, I was sure Tourmaline had been snatched into the Plant Kingdom and that was why she had never been found. The girl in the wallpaper didn't just *look* like Tourmaline. She *was* Tourmaline.

"Well," said Zenobia when I had finished. "Well."

"Well?"

"Well, it's quite a story, Elizabeth. Quite a fantastically spooky story. I especially like the part where Tourmaline is trapped—frozen!—in a world in the wallpaper."

"But you don't believe it?"

She looked at me closely. "Do *you* believe it?"

"I know it doesn't sound believable." In another room, the chimes of a clock started, and I raised my voice over the sound. "But I believe it."

Zenobia looked down at the blue-flowered eiderdown.

How could I make her believe, as I did? I tried to think, but the chiming of the clock in my ears made it impossible to concentrate.

I sat up straight. The clock! It was midnight. I fumbled for *The Plant Kingdom* by Dr. Henry Murmur and shoved it into Zenobia's hands. "Here," I said, "see for yourself."

She opened the book. "Parsley and other *Petrosilinums*," she read doubtfully.

The twelfth chime sounded.

"Turn the page," I urged.

Zenobia flicked to the next page. Her mouth made a neat O when she saw that it was covered in green, looping letters.

The little girl was happy to find herself in the Plant Kingdom. The King and Queen loved the little girl very well, and she loved them back. The King and Queen loved the little girl so well, they decided she should be crowned Princess: that she should be theirs and stay with them forever. There was only one problem. Instead of roots, the little girl had two small, pale feet. Without roots that reached down into the earth, the little girl would never be able to grow in the Plant Kingdom as she should. So the King and Queen spoke with their Council of Gardeners, and it was decided. The little girl would have roots grafted onto her legs where her feet now stood. And when the grafting was done, she would be crowned Princess.

And she would stay in the Plant Kingdom as Princess, forever and ever and ever.

My stomach twisted. Tourmaline was in terrible danger.

I leaped out of bed. "Quickly," I hissed to Zenobia, but Zenobia was already putting a new candle into the silver holder.

We hurried to the nursery in a wobbling pool of candlelight.

I found Tourmaline in the wallpaper, half-hidden by the curtain. I held up the photograph so Zenobia could see the resemblance.

"Exactly the same," she breathed. "Or they would be, if it weren't for that freckle. It's on the left cheek here in the photograph but on the right cheek in the wallpaper. And she still has both her feet."

I shone the candle over Tourmaline's feet. One was bare, one was wearing a red shoe.

"She hasn't been grafted, then," I said.

"No," said Zenobia. "Not yet."

We came back from the nursery. While the night stretched into morning, we sat wrapped in blankets and whispered about Tourmaline. Our talk came back, always, to the same two questions: how had Tourmaline gotten into the Plant Kingdom? And how could we get her out, before it was too late?

After a time, Zenobia's eyelids started to droop and her head nodded heavily. She was soon asleep.

But I stayed awake, and thin, early-morning light was starting through the window.

I closed the door on Zenobia and walked through the sleeping house, through its empty rooms and down its empty corridors, until I was outside in the misty garden.

I didn't know where I was going, but it felt good to walk. Walking settled my confused thoughts.

I went past the dead, dry flower beds, and the sundial, and the overgrown hedge maze. It made me nervous, even being near the maze, and I walked as far away from it as I could.

I went up the steep hill and looked at the fields that spread out below it. I walked down through the fields and over the stone fences that lay between them, gathering speed, until I came into Witheringe Green.

I wondered if I should turn back, but my feet were running down the narrow streets, past the haberdasher's and the seed shop. When I came to the stone church, my head caught up with where my feet were taking me.

I was going to the cemetery.

Tourmaline, said the headstone, *aged seven years. Beloved daughter of Edward and Lydia. Adored sister of Henry.*

My legs felt suddenly tired. I sat down on the grave and leaned my head against the cool stone.

If Tourmaline was grafted, she would stay in the Plant Kingdom forever. Father had been haunted all these years by her disappearance. And now I would be haunted by her, too—unless there was some way of rescuing her. But it seemed impossible. I didn't even know how Tourmaline had found her way into the Plant Kingdom in the first place, much less if there were any way of getting her out again.

My head was full of worries, and like storm clouds, those worries were growing bigger and darker. I couldn't think. I could hardly breathe.

I felt the corners of my eyes start to prick with tears.

Then I remembered what Miss Clemency had told me: when you fill your mind up with words—beautiful words, stirring words—those words drive away your worries.

I began to recite "The Lady of Shalott" as best as I could remember.

*"On either side the river lie
Long fields of barley and of rye."*

It did make me feel better, if only a little.

I stumbled over some of the words, and some lines I forgot altogether. But I kept going, verse after verse, until I came to my very favorite part.

*"Out flew the web and floated wide;
The mirror crack'd from side to side;
'The curse is come upon me,' cried
The Lady of Shalott."*

I stopped. "The mirror crack'd from side to side."

Of course!

I sprang to my feet.

In the blue guest bedroom, Zenobia mumbled the names of deadly nightshades in her sleep. "*Mandragora*," she said into her pillow. "*Datura . . . Atropa belladonna . . .*"

I shook her roughly awake.

"Mmpf?" She lifted her tousled head.

"I think I know how Tourmaline was taken into the Plant Kingdom," I said.

Zenobia sat up straight. "You do?"

"Well—no," I admitted. "I don't know. But I had an idea. And if there's any chance that I'm right, then we might somehow save Tourmaline from being—"

From being grafted, I meant to say, but the word was so terrible, it stuck in my throat.

"What's your idea, then?" Zenobia rubbed her eyes.

"I'll explain on the way," I told her, and I tossed her one of her ragged black dresses. "Here, get dressed!"

I rushed downstairs and crossed through the front room, dragging Zenobia behind me.

"The silver pool," I said as I pushed aside the floral tapestry that covered the entrance to the East Wing. "The pool that the Queen looked through into the nursery. The pool that she made with her tears. I told you about it last night, remember?"

"Oh, I remember. It struck me as poetic, in a melancholy sort of way."

I took the dusty stairs two at a time with Zenobia close behind me. I raced down the corridor lined with portraits. Then, with my hand on the nursery doorknob, I stopped.

"What if the Queen's silver pool is the mirror?" I said.

"You think," Zenobia said, "that Tourmaline went into the Plant Kingdom through the mirror?"

I nodded.

"And you think that, through the mirror, we might be able to get her out again?"

I swallowed hard. "I hope so," I said, and I opened the door.

In the nursery, I pulled the mirror away from the wall and peered behind it.

I don't know what I had expected to find there, but I didn't expect that it would only be more wallpaper. "Nothing," I said. "Just—nothing."

Tourmaline was in the same part of the wall, near the curtain, where she had been last night. Zenobia knelt there now.

"Bring me that photograph, Elizabeth," she demanded.

I handed it to her, and she held photograph–Tourmaline up next to wallpaper–Tourmaline. She studied the two side by side a long time.

At last she said, "Elizabeth, I do believe you're right. Tourmaline came to the Plant Kingdom through the mirror. Do you see here?"

She pointed at the photograph. I peered at the place her finger pointed.

"It's just a freckle," I said.

"Not *just* a freckle," said Zenobia. "In the photograph, the freckle appears on Tourmaline's left cheek. Here in the wallpaper, it appears on her right cheek."

"What does that have to do with anything?" I burst out. How was Zenobia's talk about freckles bringing us closer to saving Tourmaline?

"Don't you remember, Elizabeth? What's leftwise in real life shows rightwise in a mirror. Tourmaline is leftwise in the photograph and rightwise in the wallpaper. She *must* have come through the mirror." Zenobia grinned. "How uncommonly—and I do mean uncommonly—brilliant of you to have worked it all out."

I didn't understand what Zenobia had to grin about. What use was it knowing how Tourmaline had gotten into the Plant Kingdom if we couldn't get her out again?

"Ah," said Zenobia craftily, "but perhaps we do know a way to get her out again."

She stood up and walked to the mirror. She steadied its frame and blew directly onto its glass. The mirror's surface misted with her breath.

"I don't understand," I began, but she held up her hand to silence me. She stretched out her index finger and carefully began to write.

Across the mirror, in letters back to front, Zenobia wrote: *Tourmaline, are you there? Please talk with us.*

Zenobia turned around and smiled at me. "Occasionally— only very occasionally, mind—Miss Clemency imparts knowledge of some use."

I glanced at the place half-behind the curtain where wallpaper Tourmaline had stood. She was gone.

We watched the mirror.

Nothing happened.

Nothing happened for such a long time that I started to feel desperate. Perhaps Tourmaline hadn't seen our mirror message. Perhaps—it turned my insides cold to think about it—her grafting had already begun.

But then—

"Look," said Zenobia in a low voice, pointing. I followed her finger, not entirely sure what I was looking at.

"The mirror," she said. "It's not reflecting anymore."

She was right. My own reflection was gone. The mirror's glass rippled, like a pool of water.

I stretched out a hand but stopped short of touching the glass. I turned to Zenobia. "Should I?"

"We both will," she said. She took my hand in hers. We reached together into the mirror. Our hands plunged through the surface into liquid. I pulled away quickly. The water was freezing cold, and my hand came away covered in a thin layer of greenish slime.

Far away, at what seemed to be the bottom of the pool, a figure appeared. Her outline came to us wobbly and quavering through the water, but I could make out the wild hair, the striped dress.

"Tourmaline," I breathed.

"You should speak up." Tourmaline's voice dribbled through the water. "I can't hear you well at all."

"Tourmaline." I cupped my hands and brought my mouth as

close as I could to the mirror's liquid surface. "I need to tell you something."

"You'll have to make it quick," she said. "My coronation is starting in a few minutes."

"That's just it," I said. "You can't be Princess Tourmaline."

"Who are you?" rippled the voice. "And what do you mean, I can't be Princess?"

"I'm Elizabeth," I said, "and this is Zenobia. And we're—"

I stopped. The truth was, I didn't have the slightest idea how to explain who we were to Tourmaline.

"Visitors," Zenobia supplied. "We're visitors at Witheringe House."

"And we're sorry to tell you," I added, "but no, you can't be Princess. You simply can't. Because if you do become Princess, you'll have to stay in the Plant Kingdom forever. And you've already been away such a long time."

"It hasn't been long," came the faraway voice. "And I'll be back before dinner, or I'll be in all sorts of trouble from Father. And I don't plan to miss Henry's birthday. It's tomorrow. I have his present all wrapped. Do you want to know what it is?"

"Tourmaline, please listen—"

"But I'll only tell you if you can keep a secret. Can you?"

"It's very important, Tourmaline—"

"It's a microscope! He's going to be very pleased. And so he should—it's a very good present. Perhaps I'll get one like it when *I* turn ten."

Zenobia and I exchanged glances. "She thinks she's been there no more than a day," Zenobia muttered from the side of her mouth.

"Well," demanded Tourmaline, "do you think it's a good present or not?"

This time Zenobia put her mouth up to the mirror. "It's an excellent present. And don't you want to be sure you can give it to him? It's getting late," she lied. "It will be Henry's birthday before you know it."

"But I can't miss my coronation," she replied. "An orchestra of cicadas is going to play, and whole flocks of birds are singing. And I'm to wear a dress made out of butterfly wings and garlands of moon-flowers and glass-flowers and all kinds of other flowers that I never saw in the gardens at Witheringe House. I'm going to look quite wonderful—except for my shoe, of course."

Tourmaline dabbled her feet in the pool. One wore a red shoe. The other was muddy and bare.

"Do you see?" she asked. "I've lost my shoe. I think I'll look ever so silly, all dressed up with only one shoe on. The King says there's no need to worry about shoes—he says my feet will be taken care of. But I *would* like to have both shoes, just the same."

I looked at Zenobia helplessly. How could we convince Tourmaline of the danger she was in?

"There's no need to convince her," said Zenobia, reading my thoughts, and she reached her hand into my pocket and pulled out again the small red shoe.

"I have your other shoe, Tourmaline," Zenobia said, and she held it in front of the mirror. "Why don't you come and get it?"

"I don't think I should," said Tourmaline, doubtful.

"But you will look much better with both your red shoes," coaxed Zenobia.

"I suppose, if I'm quick about it, no one need notice," said Tourmaline. She looked around her. Then she took a breath and dived into the silver pool. She swam closer and closer to us. Her dress filled up like a balloon, and her hair fanned out around her. Bubbles streamed out of her mouth.

She reached out her hand.

Zenobia held the shoe out. But just as Tourmaline came within reach of it, Zenobia thrust her other hand through the mirror and wrapped it around Tourmaline's wrist.

Tourmaline jerked back, but Zenobia held fast. I reached elbow-deep into the mirror and took hold of Tourmaline's arm.

Together, Zenobia and I were far stronger than Tourmaline. We pulled her almost to the edge of the mirror.

But then the water started to pull her back. Pondweed wound

in ropes around her arms and legs. The plants in the wallpaper strained and pulled too, sucking her back into the Plant Kingdom.

We dug our heels into the floor and pulled Tourmaline through the mirror. Just her hands at first, all dripping with water and silt and pondweed, but then the rest of her, too, in a spill of freezing water.

There was a splintering noise and a flash—was it lightning?— of green crackled light, and somewhere, in the splintering and the crackling, the three of us tumbled onto the floor.

10
The Broken Mirror

I lay, eyes closed and head spinning, on the floor. I put my hand to my face, to my hair, to my dress. I was, to my surprise, bone dry. I sat up carefully. Tourmaline lay on the floor beside me. I reached out to touch her.

She felt warm.

She felt real.

She *was* real.

Happiness floated through me. We had done it. We had rescued Tourmaline from the Plant Kingdom, and now she was here—*really* here—with us.

Zenobia pulled herself up from the floor. She blinked heavily.

"Seven years' bad luck." She grinned, pointing to the shards of mirror scattered around us. The empty mirror frame dangled crooked on the wall. Zenobia examined the mirror fragments and picked up one that was especially sharp and curved.

"A piece of genuine misfortune," she said, holding the glass up to the light and admiring it. "I shall keep it about me as a charm."

"Charms are supposed to be *good* luck," I said. "Four-leaf clovers, horseshoes, that type of thing."

Zenobia rolled her eyes. "Elizabeth, sometimes you can be so unimaginative. Good luck is terribly cliché. Bad luck is far more exciting."

Tourmaline started to stir. She sat up and rubbed her eyes. The first thing she saw was her red shoe. She smiled widely and pushed her foot into it.

"There." She wiggled her foot proudly. "That's much better, isn't it?"

Then she saw the mirror shards. Her smile wobbled.

"Oh, no," she said. "Oh, *no*! The mirror wasn't supposed to break!"

On hands and knees she tried to put the mirror back together, but it had shattered into too many pieces.

"If the mirror's broken," she said, "I can't get back to the Plant Kingdom—and it's almost time for my coronation! I was going to wear a dress made of butterfly wings! I was going to hear the cicada orchestra play!"

She let the pieces of mirror she held fall from her hands. She looked so disappointed, I felt almost sorry for her.

"I was going to be a princess," she said sadly.

"You were *going* to have your feet cut off and tree roots tied onto your stumps," muttered Zenobia.

Tourmaline looked directly at Zenobia. "What did you say?" she asked.

Zenobia started. After all, she wasn't accustomed to anyone other than me being able to see her. But she recovered quickly. "I *said*," she snapped, "you were *going* to—"

I interrupted quickly. "What Zenobia means," I said, "is that you were in grave danger, Tourmaline, as long as you were in the Plant Kingdom."

"Danger?" said Tourmaline. "I was never in any danger. The King and Queen were as nice as could be. They were going to make me their princess."

"But that's just it, Tourmaline," I said. "They wanted to make you stay with them forever."

"I wouldn't have stayed forever," said Tourmaline. "Just until Henry's birthday."

"You wouldn't have had a choice in the matter," I said, trying to think of a way to explain.

Tourmaline looked doubtfully at her feet in their red shoes. "Why?" she asked.

"You were to be grafted," said Zenobia. "Your feet were to be cut off—snip-snap!—and your legs, or what was left of them, tied to a tree with a strong set of roots. And you would have grown into the tree and the tree would have grown into you until, in the end, you *were* the tree and the tree *was* you."

Zenobia's gruesome description turned Tourmaline pale. She looked to me and then to Zenobia and then, once more, down at her feet. "I suppose," she said, "I could stay here a while." Her face brightened. "After all, we hardly ever have visitors to Witheringe House. Especially"—she gave Zenobia a shy smile—"visitors as queer as you."

"Queer *indeed*," sniffed Zenobia.

"Oh, don't be displeased!" said Tourmaline. "I think you're just delightful!"

Zenobia blanched.

"I've never met anyone as pale or as—as *wobbly*-looking," Tourmaline continued. She grabbed Zenobia by the hand and pulled her to her feet. "Ooh!" Tourmaline shivered. "And you're just *wonderfully* cold." She dragged Zenobia to a corner of the nursery. "I could show you my toy soldiers, if you'd like."

"Elizabeth"—Zenobia's voice was strained—"will you detach this child from me?"

But I was too busy looking at the wallpaper to reply.

I wasn't imagining it. It was greener than I had seen it before. And right in front of my eyes, it was growing greener still. Now, the whole nursery was lit with a sickly green light. It bounced off the mirror shards and made strange green rainbows.

And that wasn't all.

It was *moving*.

I couldn't see it moving, but every time I blinked, the plants and vines in the paper shifted around. They crowded close to the wall, pressing against it. Almost like they wanted to get out.

"Elizabeth!" said Zenobia.

The tree was moving, as well. It was taller every time I looked at it. Its leaves reached out over all four walls of the nursery.

I looked at the lichen that sprouted like a beard from its trunk. I looked at its two big branched hands. I looked at the leaves that wound like a crown. And below the crown, I looked at the two knots of wood that looked almost like eyes.

The tree looked almost exactly like—

And then, one after the other, the two knots of wood creaked open, like eyelids.

The Plant King stared straight back at me.

"Elizabeth!" hissed Zenobia.

"We need to leave," I said. "We need to leave this room right now. Bring Tourmaline with you."

"I could hardly fail to bring her," said Zenobia, holding Tourmaline at arm's length, "as she has practically glued herself to me."

I felt better once we were outside the nursery and I had pulled the door firmly shut behind us. I felt better still once I had found, in another room off the dusty corridor, a chest of drawers covered by a dust sheet and, with Zenobia's help, had dragged it across the corridor to jam the nursery door shut.

"What are you doing?" asked Tourmaline impatiently. "I thought we were all going to play together in the nursery. I could have showed you my soldiers, or my dolls—"

"*Dolls*." Zenobia shuddered.

"Or we could have had turns on the rocking horse."

"I just thought," I said to Tourmaline, "it might be even more fun to play something out here."

"Oh," she said. "You mean an outside game!" She clapped her hands together. "I know plenty of those! We could have a round of leapfrog, if you like."

Zenobia clutched her stomach. She looked genuinely unwell.

"Or," said Tourmaline, "I could fetch some cups and saucers from the kitchen and we could play tea parties!"

"I have an idea." Zenobia's voice turned strangely pleasant. "What about a game of hide and seek?"

"No," I rushed. "No, I don't think that's a good idea at all."

Zenobia ignored me. "Tourmaline"—she smiled down at her—"you hide."

Before I could stop her, Tourmaline scampered down the hall. "I know every secret place in the whole of Witheringe House!" she called over her shoulder. "You'll never find me!"

I sprinted after her down the stairs. Tourmaline slipped

through the tapestry. When I pushed it aside and stepped into the front room, she was nowhere to be seen.

"What did you do that for?" I cried at Zenobia, who followed after me.

"You heard the girl, Elizabeth," she said. "Playing at tea parties—what a monstrous suggestion! Something had to be done."

"Now we've no idea where she is." I started pulling aside curtains and peering under armchairs.

"That was rather the point," said Zenobia. "She was starting to irritate me."

"Help me look, Zenobia!"

"I fail to see why you're so desperate to find Tourmaline. She's not in the Plant Kingdom anymore. She's safe now."

"But what if she's not safe? I think she could still be in danger." I started to tear the cushions frantically from the sofa.

Zenobia took a pink brocade cushion from my hands. "And why would you think that?"

"Because of something I saw in the nursery. The wallpaper was very green—"

"That's hardly unusual," said Zenobia.

"And it seemed to me that all the plants and vines and flowers were moving around."

Zenobia frowned.

"That's not all," I said. "There was a tree in the wallpaper, too. A tree with big branched hands and a lichen beard and a crown of thick dark leaves and"—my voice was soft as a whisper now—"and *eyes*," I said. "I think it was the Plant King. I think he wants Tourmaline back."

"But he's not going to get her back, is he?" she reasoned. "Not as long as he's on one side of the wallpaper and she's on the other."

"I'm not so sure," I said, and I pointed to a patch of wall behind Zenobia's head. The wallpaper in the front room was cream satin with a pale pink stripe. But, crawling out from a part of the wall hidden by a grandfather clock, I saw a flash of green: a tiny, coiled vine shoot.

Zenobia put her shoulder to the clock and started to push it away from the wall. I saw what she meant to do, and I leaned in against the clock's mahogany case, too. When there was a large enough space between the clock and the wall, we peered into the gap.

Here, the wallpaper was vivid green. Its pink and cream satin stripes were overgrown with thick green grass and glittering green flowers.

My stomach sank.

The Plant Kingdom was growing, creeping, spreading through the walls of the house.

———————◆———————

"Tourmaline!"

"Tourmaline!"

"You can come out now, Tourmaline!"

"Stop hiding, Tourmaline!"

We raced through the rooms of the house, calling her name.

In the music room, we lifted the lid off the grand piano and looked for her among its strings.

In the schoolroom, we pulled the atlases and encyclopedias from their shelves to check she wasn't hidden behind them.

In the parlor, we overturned the ottomans and upset the tea trolley.

We crawled under the dining room table and even turned up the carpets in the hope that Tourmaline had somehow concealed herself beneath them.

But she was nowhere to be found.

And everywhere we went, the Plant Kingdom followed, creeping and crawling through the wallpaper, turning it green.

Finally, we burst into the front room once more. We stood, gathering our breath.

The wallpaper plants around us grew thicker and thicker. I started to wonder if I would ever see Tourmaline again.

"Of course you'll see her again," snapped Zenobia. "We only need to find her."

"We wouldn't need to find her if *you* hadn't told her to run off and hide."

"In my defense, Elizabeth, she had proposed a game of leapfrog—"

I interrupted Zenobia. "That's no reason to—"

She interrupted me right back. "I don't know what leapfrog is—"

Now she was making me really angry. "Of all the thoughtless things—"

"And I certainly don't intend to find out—"

Before our bickering could explode into a proper argument, a tearing sound came from above us. Plaster flakes rained down onto the carpet.

A thick green vine had pushed right through the wallpaper. It crawled up along the ceiling. And it wrapped itself through the chandelier before our eyes.

"It's coming out of the wall," I breathed, half in wonder, half in fright. "It's coming in here."

The air split with the crack of shattered porcelain. The palm trees were growing out of their ornamental pots, sending showers of soil across the floor. Their trunks sprouted up. Soon their fronds reached the ceiling.

Grasses, blooming with wildflowers, sprouted up from the fibers of the Persian carpet.

And over all four walls, leafy tendrils started to slither out from the wallpaper. They twined around chairs and tables. They swallowed up the grandfather clock.

I stood as if glued to the spot.

I felt a cold hand wrap over mine. "We need to find Tourmaline," said Zenobia grimly. "And quickly."

We waded through the grass. It grew as high as my waist and rustled when I walked through it. Zenobia pulled me free when a sheaf of grass coiled itself around my ankle. Then I untangled Zenobia when she got caught in a thicket of vivid purple wildflowers. "Ugh," she said, shaking their tendrils from her. "*Flowers*. Hurry, get them off me!"

Finally, we were through the grass. We started up the staircase. I hoped we would find Tourmaline somewhere on the second floor. And I hoped the Plant Kingdom wouldn't follow us.

But we had only climbed the first few steps when the banisters on either side of us became slender-branched saplings. They grew taller and wider. By the time we reached the top, the staircase was shaded by a grove of trees.

We ran from room to room looking for Tourmaline. The plants followed close behind. We came into the library. "Tourmaline!" I called. "Tourmaline, please come out!" My voice was raw from yelling.

I looked for her in the corridors between shelves and behind Father's desk and under the globe of the world. Zenobia spread her hands wide and shook her head. She hadn't found her either.

There was a low, rumbling sound. We stood and watched as, one by one, the bookshelves lining the walls warped and twisted and grew branches and leaves, until we were standing in a forest where books grew like fruit from the trees.

We edged out of the library and down the corridor, until we came to the flagstone staircase that led down to the kitchen.

Zenobia started down the steps. I took one last look over my shoulder at the thickening forest, then followed her.

At the door to the kitchen, Zenobia hesitated. Perhaps she was wondering, like I was, what we would find behind it.

With a burst of resolve, she pushed the door open.

The kitchen, it seemed, was safe from the Plant Kingdom. Sunlight fell through its windows and onto the copper pots that bubbled on the stove and the strings of onions and frilled heads of cabbage that lay on the table.

And while the rest of the house was filled with the rustling of grass and leaves and the creaking of tree branches, here it was quiet. Almost silent.

Almost.

Zenobia tilted her head toward the bread basket and lifted one eyebrow.

I moved closer.

From the basket came the soft but unmistakable sound of a small high voice, humming to itself.

I lifted the basket to see Tourmaline, covered in flour and wearing a wide smile on her face.

"What did I tell you?" she said. "I know all the very best places to hide!"

I squeezed Tourmaline's hands. "I'm so glad we found you," I said.

"Well of course," said Tourmaline. "That's how the game works."

"Elizabeth." Zenobia's voice was low and tight. "Look."

A vine was pushing through the gap between the door and the floor.

It was only a slim tendril, but it was crawling very fast over the flagstone floor. And it was reaching out toward Tourmaline.

I looked around wildly for a way out, and I spied a door that led outside. "Into the garden," I said, and we tumbled out into sunshine.

At least the Plant Kingdom hadn't crept into the garden. The trees and bushes here were just as dead and gray as ever. Even the weeds were well behaved.

"It's a beautiful day, isn't it?" Tourmaline tugged on Zenobia's hand. "And look at those fluffy white clouds! See how that one looks like a pony? And that one there is exactly like a Christmas tree!"

"If she says one more word to me about *clouds*," hissed Zenobia, "I will cut off her feet myself."

I looked back at the house. Most of its windows had been smashed by branches. Vines as thick as rope were wrapped around it. They had dislodged one of the stone gargoyles that I so disliked and toppled it to the ground, where it now lay in pieces.

The house looked like Sleeping Beauty's castle, only the bushes here had not taken a hundred years to grow—they had sprung up in minutes.

"And that cloud over *there*," I heard Tourmaline say, "looks like a sweet little—oh! Oh!"

I spun around.

My heart clenched.

The dead garden was filled with life.

Dry gray grass shot up around us. Trees pressed close and blotted out the sun. Weeds and thistles slithered over our feet and pulled at our ankles.

Only a narrow path in front of us was free of overgrown weeds.

Before we could decide if we wanted to follow it or not, the earth rose up, rippling with tree roots, under our feet and sent us falling forward onto the path.

Tourmaline, bewildered, started to run. Zenobia ran after her and I followed, running as fast as I could until I saw where the path was taking us.

I stopped dead.

"Wait!" I cried.

We were heading for the hedge maze. It was even thicker now, even more tangled. Its hedge, once bare, was covered in dark, spiky leaves. The same dark, spiky leaves that wound, like a crown, around the tree that was growing up, up, up, and showing no sign of stopping, from the center of the maze.

"Wait!" I yelled even louder now. "Come back!"

Zenobia turned. She pulled Tourmaline back with her.

"Don't you see?" I said. I pointed up at the tree, at its crown, at the two branches that were growing like arms out either side of its trunk.

Zenobia looked around her. "Follow me," she said, and she crouched and pushed aside an armful of dense undergrowth, making a gap just wide enough to crawl through.

We slithered along on our bellies. Zenobia went first, and I went last, with Tourmaline in between. Twigs snagged in my hair. Rocks pierced my palms. My mouth filled with dirt.

At last we reached a place where the garden didn't grow quite as quickly.

"We're nearly free," said Zenobia. Her voice came back to me in ragged snatches. "I see the nursery up ahead. Perhaps we'll be safe there."

But before I could reply, I found myself caught on a branch. I shouted for Zenobia, but she and Tourmaline had run ahead.

As I fumbled myself free of the thorny branch, I squinted back down at the garden. The Plant Kingdom had swallowed up nearly half of the hill. When I looked the other way, I saw a thin strip of garden that was still free and, perched on the edge of the hill, the nursery. Zenobia and Tourmaline grew smaller and smaller the closer they came to it.

I remembered the last time I was in the nursery. I remembered the red shoe. I remembered the very special grafting the gardener had been practicing. And the way he had sharpened the shears. And his words to me, as I went out the door. "I'll see you again before too long, Miss Elizabeth."

And, all at once, I understood. Tourmaline was in terrible danger.

"Stop!" I cried after them. "Stop!"

But Zenobia and Tourmaline were very far away by now. Before my voice could reach them, it was carried away on the wind.

11

The Hedge Maze

With my hands pressed against the soil-streaked windows, I peered into the nursery. Inside, the plants were neatly ordered, contained in pots and planters. The worktable, usually covered in seedlings and cuttings, was bare except for a film of dirt, the rusted shears, and a green shrub that had been pulled from its pot. The plant's leaves were flat against the tabletop. Its dense network of roots reached like a hand into the air.

The gardener stood behind the table.

I needed to warn Zenobia about the gardener. I needed to get Tourmaline out of the nursery. I needed to do both these things without the gardener seeing me. But he was facing the door. So I stayed where I was and waited for my chance.

I watched the gardener talking with Zenobia and Tourmaline,

with a smile oozing over his face. I watched him opening his shears. I watched him slice the shrub's roots from its leafy top. When sap dribbled over his glove, and he turned away to shake it clean, I saw my chance. I eased the door open. It moved so softly on its hinges, it was nearly silent. I slipped inside.

I crept around behind the gardener, trying to catch Zenobia's eye. But she was looking, transfixed, at the gardener.

"I can assure you," he was saying, "you'll both be safe as long you're here in the nursery." He turned to Zenobia. "I believe we have met before." Then he looked at Tourmaline. "But I don't believe *we've* been introduced."

"Tourmaline Murmur," said Tourmaline, and she held her hand out to the gardener.

The gardener stepped out from behind the table to take it.

As he did, I heard a churning sound. I looked down. In the place where the gardener should have had feet, he had roots.

My heart pounded.

Tourmaline saw none of this.

She looked up at the gardener and smiled.

And that was when I should have leaped forward and pulled Tourmaline out of reach, or launched myself at the gardener and knocked him to the ground, or at least yelled out some kind of warning.

That was what I had come into the nursery to do.

But I did none of those things. I stood stuck to the spot. I couldn't make myself move or speak. My legs didn't work. My mouth didn't work.

I was frozen through with fear.

The gardener removed his glove to show a knobbled hand that sprouted five green ribbony fingers.

Tourmaline's smile wavered.

I needed to do something. But, still, I didn't move.

The gardener wrapped his ribbony fingers around Tourmaline's arm. "It's a pleasure to meet you, Princess," he said. Then he hefted her up and flung her onto the table.

Plants pushed out of their pots. They crawled away from their trellises and broke through their soil beds. They reached out their tendrils toward Tourmaline.

And now, for the first time since we had pulled her from the Plant Kingdom, Tourmaline understood the danger she was in.

The gardener meant to graft her.

Tourmaline's shriek rattled the nursery walls. But not for long. Green tendrils wrapped around her arms and legs and bound her to the worktable. Flowers covered her eyes and filled her mouth, muffling her cries. Vines covered her like a cocoon.

Soon all that could be seen of Tourmaline were her two feet in their red shoes.

The gardener opened the shears and brought them toward Tourmaline's ankles.

Until now, Zenobia had watched in horror, just like me. But now she flew at the gardener, ragged and black and shrieking like a raven. She clawed at his eyes and stomped over his roots. The gardener stumbled back. The shears fell from his hands.

I stood watching, admiring and ashamed.

Admiring the swift, fearless way Zenobia sprang to Tourmaline's rescue.

And ashamed of myself for shrinking into a corner.

The gardener set himself upright again. He wrapped his green fingers around Zenobia's throat. "You're making a nuisance of yourself," he said.

"I won't let you do it!" sputtered Zenobia. "I won't let you graft her! It's too cruel!"

"Perhaps it is cruel," said the gardener. "Certainly, it will be painful. But the Plant King has given his orders."

"Why should you follow them?" choked Zenobia. "You're not in the Plant Kingdom."

"Ah, but there you're wrong. Wherever the Plant King is, so is his Kingdom. And he's growing. Can't you feel it? He's nearly here." And he pushed Zenobia up against a trellis.

Green tendrils pushed their way over the ground.

They twined around Zenobia's ankles.

It was too awful. I couldn't watch. I looked at the ground instead.

The shears lay in the dirt. Without the shears, surely there could be no grafting. And if I could take the shears, unnoticed . . .

The tendrils crept up to Zenobia's waist. They tied her arms tightly against the trellis. She wriggled and cursed, but she couldn't free herself.

Slowly, I stretched out a hand and eased the shears toward me.

Zenobia was now almost as covered in green as Tourmaline was. All I could see of her was the black glint of her eyes.

I flashed her a look. It was a look meant to say that she shouldn't worry. That I had a plan.

And it was true, I did have a plan.

But it was a brave plan. And it needed someone braver than me to make it work.

Zenobia looked back at me through the vines covering her face. If she was surprised to see me, she didn't show it. And she didn't seem surprised when I picked up the shears, either. Instead, her eyes sparkled. She looked as if she were proud of me.

I edged out of the nursery, and though I hated leaving Zenobia and Tourmaline there, I shut the door behind me.

I knew what I had to do.

The tree that grew from the center of the maze was very tall now. Its crown was thick and green. Its branched arms reached out wide.

I ran toward the maze as fast as I could, pushing through thorny bushes and tangled grass.

The gardener sped after me. His roots churned through the soil, bringing up sprays of dirt. The branches that had hindered me bent to let him pass. I put my head down and gritted my teeth. And ran faster. The slope turned steep under my feet, and I ran faster still. Then I skidded, stumbled, and fell face-first into scratchy hedge.

I was at the entrance to the maze.

Wherever the Plant King is, the gardener had said, so is his Kingdom. If I could destroy the Plant King, maybe I could set Tourmaline free.

I peered inside. The maze was even darker, and even more choking, than I had remembered it. The tree at its center looked, to me, at least twice as tall as the house.

I hesitated a moment. Could I do it?

It was a moment too long.

I felt ribbony fingers on my shoulder.

I forced the shears open and whipped around to face the gardener.

"Don't move," I told him, "or I'll cut your fingers clean off!" My words were brave but my voice shook.

"Go on, then." He waggled his fingers at me. "Cut away."

I swallowed. I lifted the shears. But then I let them fall down again.

The gardener laughed. "I knew you wouldn't do it. You're not a brave girl, Elizabeth. Now, return the shears to me and you won't be harmed."

"And Tourmaline? Will she be harmed? I know what you mean to do to her," I said.

"Tourmaline will live as a princess," he said, "in a green and happy kingdom."

"Tourmaline belongs *here*," I said.

"And why would you have her stay here?" He sneered. "Is it really such a happy place? Are *you* happy here?"

My throat grew tight. My eyes brimmed with tears. But I held fast to the shears.

"Well, then," he said, "I shall graft you, too. The Plant Kingdom would be glad to have you."

He eased his ribbony fingers toward the shears. "And besides . . ." He came closer. "It's not like anyone would miss you. No one would even notice you were gone."

And there it was. My deepest and most secret fear. Greater than all my other fears together, the small ones (gargoyles, gloves without hands in them) and the large ones (ghosts, the twisty, turning hedge maze). The fear that I was invisible and unloved.

But there is one good thing about hearing your deepest fear spoken out loud—nothing else that made you afraid before will ever seem so large or so terrible again. Not even a deep, scary maze. Not even the dark, twisty tree waiting, like a monster, at its center.

"No," I said. My voice came out loud and strong and clear. "I'll never go with you. And I won't let you take Tourmaline, either!"

And I turned and ran into the maze.

I ran through the maze in twists and turns. But the gardener seemed to know where my feet would take me even before I did. I felt him close behind me, churning up the path with his roots.

I ran faster.

The hedge rustled. Quiet at first, but the noise grew louder with every step I took. The spiky leaves that covered the hedge were growing bigger and bigger. Some were as big as saucers, some as big as dinner plates. I heard a crack. The tree's two branched arms split and twisted at their ends into two dark hands that grabbed angrily at the air.

Over the rustling, I heard the gardener's voice close behind me. "One small, trembling girl is no match for the Plant King."

I didn't care. I kept running.

The leaves around me grew thicker. They pressed in on either side of me. They blocked out the sun. I groped through the strangling, scratching dark, choking back tears.

And then I stumbled into the clearing at the center of the maze.

The tree had sprouted a lichen beard, which crawled with worms and beetles. A gash, crusted with sap, split its bark in the shape of a mouth. It had two knotted whorls of wood above the gash-mouth, in the place where eyes would be. Its roots had swelled and grown strong, and they reached down into the soil. I knew I had to cut its roots.

I felt very small and very scared. But I opened the shears with shaking hands, and I ran toward the tree. I brought the blades together around one of the roots and tried to snap it through. But it was thick and wiry, and no matter how hard I tried, I couldn't force the shears through it.

Above me, I felt the tree twist and bend.

One of the knotted eyes cracked open. The mouth let out a deep, earthy roar, and the branched hands swiped at me.

I squeezed the shears even tighter.

I cut the root in two.

And as the root split, the tree withered and shriveled—only a little, but enough to give me hope. I cut through another root and another.

Soon, the ground around me was littered with snapped roots, and the tree was growing smaller and more shriveled and less like the Plant King.

And then I heard a churning sound behind me.

The gardener.

"I admire your persistence, Elizabeth," came his snaky voice, "but you can't possibly defeat the Plant King. I won't allow it."

I felt his ribbony fingers tight around my leg. And he brought me to the ground with a thud. I kept my grip on the shears tight and wriggled out of the gardener's grasp.

The Plant King was weakening. The gardener was wrong—I could defeat him, if I could only cut a few more roots.

But, one by one, the root stumps around me were finding their way back into the ground. I felt the Plant King growing stronger in the tree, turning it taller and more powerful.

I wrenched the shears open once more, but before I could cut another root, I felt something coil around my rib cage. Roots were wrapping themselves around me. They squeezed tight. I felt my bones start to buckle. They squeezed tighter. They pushed the air out of my chest.

I couldn't breathe.

My eyes blurred. The shears fell from my hands.

And then, just as everything turned to black, I felt a chill and something cold brush past me.

There was a loud snap. The roots released their grip on me, and I tumbled to the ground. I stayed there a while, on my hands and knees, taking in deep gulps of air, until an icy hand took my arm and lifted me to my feet.

In front of me stood Zenobia.

"Zenobia?" I asked. "How did you get free?"

She smiled and held out the sharp sliver of mirror. "Fortunately, I had my bad luck charm about me." She lifted the shard above her head and brought it down on another of the Plant King's roots. It severed easily. The Plant King groaned as one of his branched arms drooped, then withered away to nothing.

The gardener's face twisted with rage. He stretched his fingers wide and lunged at the shears, which lay in the dirt where I had dropped them. I fell to my knees, scrambling to get to them first. The gardener's ribbony fingers brushed over mine, but I was too quick.

Only one root connected the Plant King tree with the soil now. I opened the shears and brought the blades together hard around it.

The root snapped clean in two.

A green-white flash of light filled my eyes, and a loud splintering filled my ears. When I looked again, the tree was just a tree. It was split and charred as if it had been struck by lightning, though the sky was as blue and clear as it had been before.

I pulled myself up. The hedge was still. Its dark green leaves were neat and ordered.

The gardener was nowhere to be seen.

The Plant King was gone.

I looked down at the shears in my hand. The Plant King was gone, because of *me*.

Zenobia cleared her throat. "Not *all* because of you, Elizabeth. Though"—she sounded almost admiring—"I suppose you were a little magnificent."

We made our way out of the maze and climbed up to the top of the hill. From there, we could see all the way down to the house. I cupped my hands over my eyes and squinted through the sunshine. "It looks—it looks *normal!*" I cried. "And the garden—"

Zenobia patted my arm. "Don't fret over the garden, Elizabeth. The Plant Kingdom, it seems, has gone. The house is as it was before, from the outside, at least. It is a shame that the garden has lost its witheredness, but sometimes these things can't be helped."

"But I *like* the garden," I said. It was covered in a soft wash of green. Trees and bushes that had been gray and dead before were lush with leaves. The dry, moth-eaten rose garden had bloomed. The air smelled of flowers and honey.

Zenobia sniffed. "Well," she said, "there's no accounting for taste." She turned on her heel and made for the nursery shed.

I followed after her, feeling my heart lift up with happiness. But it sank like a stone when we pushed open the door.

The worktable was strewn with dry and withered tendrils, but Tourmaline was nowhere to be seen. We sifted through the stalks and leaves. We searched the nursery up and down. We ran through the garden calling her name.

But Tourmaline was gone.

12

The Plant Kingdom

by

Dr. Henry Murmur

Afer we had combed every inch of the garden, we went back to the house to search for Tourmaline. Inside, there was no trace of the Plant Kingdom. It was as if it had never been in the house at all. The rooms were still. Our footsteps were the only sounds to break the silence.

We went from room to room. The schoolroom was empty. The library and the nursery were, too. Tourmaline wasn't in the East Wing, and she wasn't in the West Wing, either. I started to think we might not find her at all.

I sat on the carpet in the front room and looked at its fabric flowers. We had gone through every room in Witheringe House. And each of them had been empty.

I felt hollow. We had defeated the Plant King, but we had somehow lost Tourmaline.

Zenobia sat beside me. She looked as dejected as I felt.

I edged my fingers across the carpet until they brushed hers. Zenobia gave a pained sigh. But she didn't take her hand away.

A door creaked and shuddered.

I leaped to my feet, half-hoping . . .

But it was Father, not Tourmaline. Miss Clemency followed him. Her hands were filled with bright wildflowers.

The hope drained out of me.

I must have looked very sad, because Father put a gentle hand on my head and stroked my hair. I wrapped my arms around him in a hug, and after a pause, he hugged me back.

"Is everything all right, Elizabeth?" he asked when I pulled free. His face was concerned. "Has something happened?"

So much had happened. But I didn't know where I would begin telling it all to Father.

"No," I said. "Nothing's happened."

"Then why are you in such a state?"

I looked down at myself. My dress was splotched with dirt and grass stains. It was nearly black around the hem. My arms were covered in scratches, and my hair—I could feel it—was stuck through with twigs and leaves and strands of spiderweb.

"Mrs. Purswell," called Father.

She appeared instantly. "Yes, Dr. Murmur?"

Zenobia gaped at her. "Unbelievable," she said to herself. "Quite simply unbelievable."

"Please have a bath drawn for Elizabeth," Father told her. "And quickly. Our guest arrives at three."

In the bathroom, Zenobia sat on the rim of the tub while I worked myself clean with a sponge. Filth and soap scum filmed on the bath's surface. The water grew lukewarm, then cold around me, as I sat wondering what had happened to Tourmaline. I felt I had failed her. And I had failed Father, too. I had wanted to make him happy, and now he never could be. Not completely.

Faint music floated up from downstairs.

I tipped my head and listened. I was sure I had hidden that record under the library carpet.

"Is that—" I asked.

"It is," Zenobia nodded. "The aria from *The Magic Flute*."

I splashed my way out of the bath, wriggled my way into the clean clothes Mrs. Purswell had laid out for me, and started down the stairs.

I burst into the parlor and ripped the record from the gramophone. The conversation stopped.

"You mustn't hear that!" I told Father. My voice was ragged and my breathing was short. I saw Miss Clemency seated across from him. Her eyes went large looking at me.

I started to explain. "He mustn't hear anything from—"

"Elizabeth," said Father as he took the record from me, placed it on the gramophone, and started the music again. "I appreciate your concern. It's true I may not love Mozart, but it happens that Miss Clemency—"

"Please," Miss Clemency addressed her shoes, "call me Adelaide."

Father's cheeks tinged pink beneath his whiskers. "Adelaide is quite partial to him," he continued. "And so is—"

"But surely this must be Elizabeth!" A voice came from the other side of the room. A tall woman, with wild, curling hair that fell to her shoulders, sat in an armchair in a corner. She wore a silk dress as brightly patterned as butterfly wings. From under its hem peeked a pair of red shoes.

"So is your aunt Tourmaline," finished Father.

My breath caught in my throat.

"Elizabeth?" asked Miss Clemency. "Are you feeling well? You look as if you'd seen a ghost!"

I felt, in a way, as if I had.

Tourmaline was grown now, and her face was older. But her eyes were the very same eyes I had seen peering out of the wall-paper in the nursery. She came over to me and bent forward so her face was level with mine. She took both my hands in hers. "I feel I know you already," she said.

"Yes," I said in a dazed way. "I feel I know you, too."

"Your face"—she narrowed her eyes and, with half a smile dancing on her lips, looked closely at me—"your face is so *familiar.*"

"Sit down, won't you, Elizabeth?" said Father. "Mrs. Purs-well will be in soon with the tea."

I sank into an armchair. Zenobia perched beside me wearing a thrilled expression.

I felt like I was in a dream. Or maybe everything that came before now had been the dream? Had we really saved Tourmaline from the Plant Kingdom? Or had I just imagined it all? Father always said I had an overactive imagination.

"What perfect nonsense," snorted Zenobia. "You know very well you're not as imaginative as all that. It was entirely real."

"I know you must be right," I said. "And yet there's no sign the Plant Kingdom was ever here. Everything is just as it was—almost as if none of it ever happened."

Zenobia sighed. "I know you're not especially perceptive, Elizabeth, but surely even you can sense how the atmosphere in Witheringe House has shifted. Before, the house had a terribly gloomy, haunted feeling—a most appealing feeling, if you ask me. Now"—she wrinkled her nose in distaste—"it's light, and bright, and"—she flinched—"*happy*."

I looked around. The house was somehow brighter. Like all the shadows and sadness that had filled it had been lifted away.

Father was brighter, too. His eyes shone when he looked at Tourmaline.

"Your aunt Tourmaline," he was saying now, "has been away for a long time."

"Your aunt is a famous entomologist," Miss Clemency said. "Her work is a little like your father's, only she studies insects rather than plants."

"Yes," said Father, "Tourmaline's been away since before you were born. Traveling, as it turns out, in the jungles of Borneo, Peru—all kinds of places."

"Yes," she said lightly, "it was like being in another world."

"I suppose you saw lots of interesting plants," I said.

"The strangest plants you could ever imagine! Even if I could describe them to you, I'm not sure you'd believe they were real."

"I think I would," I said.

She laughed and leaned close to me. "But may I confess something, Elizabeth? I've never really cared for plants. They're so *green*, so *creeping*." She shuddered. "I much prefer insects."

"And I must say," said Miss Clemency, "your aunt Tourmaline has brought back some quite fascinating specimens!"

Laid out on a low, polished table were butterflies and moths behind glass, and beetles with jewel-colored carapaces, along with sketches of hairy spiders and pincered ants and other creatures I recognized as insects but whose names I didn't know.

The door creaked open, and Mrs. Purswell came in carrying a tea tray. Tourmaline sprang up. "That looks awfully heavy, Mrs. Purswell. Let me help." She took a pile of saucers and set one for each of us. "One," she said, "two, three, and four." She placed a pink porcelain saucer before me with a flourish. But she still held one in her hand. She frowned at it. "There's one too many," she said.

Father cleared his throat. "Actually," he said, "there's just enough. I think you'll find that one is for Zenobia. She usually sits beside Elizabeth."

I stared at Father, open-mouthed. He looked down at the plate of biscuits in his hands, and then he looked up at me again.

"Yes," he said gruffly. "Well, Miss Clemency and I—that is, Adelaide and I—have spoken on the matter, and Adelaide has brought me to see that Zenobia is . . . Zenobia is a good friend to you, Elizabeth. And that I haven't been as welcoming toward her as I could be. I shall try to do better, if she'll let me."

"I appreciate it," I told him warmly. "*We* appreciate it."

I turned with a smile to Zenobia. But she was absorbed in one of Tourmaline's specimens: a black beetle with long, spindled claws and antennae. "Look at this." She turned over the card it was pinned to. "An Algerian death beetle. Did you ever see such fierce pincers," she breathed, "such black beady eyes? It's quite the loveliest thing I've ever seen. Entomology *has* always struck me as a fascinating subject. I wonder why I haven't made a study of it before."

"Zenobia," said Tourmaline thoughtfully. "It's not a common name, is it?"

"Rather uncommon, actually," said Miss Clemency, and she gave me a twinkling smile.

"And yet," said Tourmaline, "I feel as if I've heard it somewhere before."

She looked directly at Zenobia as she placed the teacup before her. It was almost as if she could see Zenobia was there.

Zenobia was too busy admiring the beetle to notice, but I flashed Tourmaline a shy smile, and she smiled broadly back.

Then she turned back to the insects on the table. "Of course, all I've done all these years," she said, "is collect specimens. I haven't been as industrious as you, Henry. Look at all these books you've written!"

A stack of Father's books sat by Tourmaline's chair. She began, one by one, to pick them up and leaf through them.

"*Musings on Myrophilium* by Dr. Henry Murmur." She flipped the blue-bound book over in her hands. "*The Complete Wildflower Encyclopedia: Asphodel–Zinnia* by Dr. Henry Murmur," she said as she picked up another.

The next book she took from the pile had an earthy-brown cover. Its title was etched in green letters. "*The Plant Kingdom* by Dr. Henry Murmur," she said. "Your very first book, wasn't it, Henry?"

Father nodded. Tourmaline placed the book on the table and lifted the next one from the pile.

I reached for *The Plant Kingdom* and opened it. I was search-
ing for a sign—perhaps a sentence in looping green letters—to
show that the Plant Kingdom had been real.

I flipped through the book.

All I saw were lines of black type and dense illustrations of
nettles and dandelions.

Disappointed, I let the book drop into my lap. It fell open at
the very first page. The dedication.

I read it once.

I sat up straight.

I read it again.

"Father?"

Father and Miss Clemency and Tourmaline were all exclaim-
ing over the bright blue color of a scarab beetle, but Father set
the beetle down when I said his name.

"Yes, Elizabeth?"

"The dedication, at the start of *The Plant Kingdom*," I said.
"Was it always there?"

"Yes," he said.

"And is it—is it *true*?"

"Of course it's true," he said, and under his stern moustache,
his mouth turned up in a small smile. "Of course it is."

He turned back to Tourmaline, who was holding the scarab
up to the light, and to Miss Clemency, who was leaning in to

admire the vivid colors across the beetle's thorax. Beside me, Zenobia was still entranced by the Algerian death beetle.

I watched them a while, and then I went back to the book in my lap. Zenobia was right. Not everything was just as it had been, after all. I traced my finger over the words on the page as I read the dedication a third time.

To my daughter, Elizabeth, whom I love
more than anything in the world.

ACKNOWLEDGMENTS

Thank you to all at Text, above all to Jane, who shaped this story so deftly; to Susan and Amulet Books; to early and attentive readers, Poppy, Zoe, and Robyn; to the Miller and Brereton families; to friends in Australia and Germany and elsewhere; and, of course, to Tim.

ABOUT THE AUTHOR

Jessica Miller is an Australian writer. She was born in London, spent most of her life in Brisbane, and now lives in Berlin, where she writes books and studies German. *Elizabeth and Zenobia*, which was short-listed for the Text Prize, is her first novel.